THE OATHING STONE

J.Z.N. MCCAULEY

BOOK TWO OF THE RITUALS TRILOGY

J.Z.N. MCCAULEY

Published by White Moon Press

Illustration by Mélanie Delon | www.melaniedelon.com
Developmental Edit by Rachel Small
Edited by Candace Kuhn
Proofread by Lavender Prose

Hardcover ISBN: 9781619848290
Paperback ISBN: 9781642370034
eISBN: 9781540157812

Library of Congress Control Number: 2017960306

Printed in the United States of America

To the Rose of Sharon–for your passionate truth, unconditional love, and your unfailing justice.

To my husband and children–my best friends, soulmates, and loves of my life and beyond.

Faerie footprints are specks of magic that the earth couldn't bear to part with.

CONTENTS

1

THE WHITE LACE draped over the cool white satin on Catherine's skin, leaving her delightfully breathless in the form-fitting wedding gown. While standing in the back room belonging to one of many shops owned by Mary, her dear friend who was busying herself just in front of her, she waited patiently for her to finish the adjustments.

"It's just what I wanted," Catherine sighed with bliss, running her hands down the fabric.

Mary handed some extra fabric to her young assistant. "Aye, that's grand," she said. With two silver combs holding her snowy waves back to let fall behind her shoulders, she turned and briefly looked up at Catherine with two perceptive blue eyes that seemed to have knowledge of the whole world sitting just behind them. A few pins stuck out of one side of her mouth. "Such a gorgeous bride, Caty. Vintage styles really suit you." She fumbled to pick up a pin that had slipped out of the fabric. "Do you think the old man will like it?"

Catherine had gotten used to hearing Mary call her fiancé an old man. After all, a two-thousand-year-old druid doctor warranted such a nickname. Even though he started aging normally again shortly after Catherine first met him, and his physical appearance was the vibrant age range of mid-twenties, his revealingly deep eyes always gave away the old soul behind them. Unlike her, Mary had known right away. The nickname was always in fun, and Catherine liked that it would coax a chuckle out of Bowen. The rich yet uplifting sound set her stomach aflutter each time she heard it.

Catherine raised her eyebrows. "I hope so. What do you think?"

"He will. Aye, no man could resist."

"Are you sure it'll be ready in time?"

"Have I ever let you down? Just a few adjustments and I'll have it done well before. No need to worry your pretty red head over it."

Catherine smirked. "All right, I just can't help feeling anxious," she said, wringing her hands. "I want everything to go perfectly."

"And it will, my girl. Let things flow as they do and you'll be happier for it," Mary said.

A faint snipping sound registered before Catherine felt a sudden stinging pain coming from her ankle. "Ouch!" She bent down to see dark drops of blood speckling her dress. She gasped. "What the hell?"

"Damn, I'm sorry. I flinched when I was trying to cut underneath the train. Did I hurt you?" Mary asked, examining the cut.

Mary's assistant hurried over with a damp cloth. Catherine winced as the girl dabbed at the wound. "Don't worry about that. What about the stains?"

"Now, Caty, I'll handle it," Mary said. "I'm finished anyway. Take it off, and I'll see to those stains before you have a chance to dwell on it."

After carefully removing herself from the elegant wedding gown, Catherine was practically pushed out of the room and out into the thrift shop. A few onlookers eyed her curiously. She could feel her reddened cheeks giving away her state of mind, and hurried out of the shop.

Walking quickly through and past the small village, Catherine slowed her pace as she went up a rolling trail overgrown with tall prodding grass beside the trampled, narrow footpath she followed. She stopped often to throw her head back and soak in every ounce of sun. For once, layers of Irish clouds weren't encroaching on it. Despite her fair and sensitive skin, she knew she wouldn't burn. She had magic now and the powerful sun-shared fire within her. She was the sun, and the sun was her, and the sun loved her. Deep in her bones, she loved it too, and she could feel it sate her body's hunger for rejuvenating power like water poured over desert land. Lamentably, she and the sun could only share this connection when the skies allowed. She felt the energizing rays only in spurts through dark clouds and drizzle.

Unfortunately, the pain in her ankle kept interrupting her joy. The top of her shoe rubbed relentlessly against the cut, her ankle socks providing no protection whatsoever. Mary's house was just up ahead, and she could already smell all of the different scents of the many colorful flowers she knew skirted the outside grounds. To make sure she wouldn't be seen using magic, she would use them to her advantage. When she reached the red and brown cottage she now called home, she crouched down behind a three-foot-tall climbing Rosa canina shrub in the front garden, and rolled up her pant leg. The blood had clotted at last, but the insufficient bandage she'd just removed had done little to keep it from running.

After removing her shoe and sock, Catherine held out her right hand, palm up. Staring into it, she lightly blew out the faintest of breaths. Her palm instantly flared with red fire. She enclosed the flame against her cut, holding it there for a few seconds, and then pulled her hand away to examine her now flawless skin. The fire disappeared, leaving only tiny wisps of rising smoke as evidence of its occurrence.

Catherine rose up from behind the pale pink and white flowers, carefully avoiding their prickly hooked stems, and entered the small cottage in search of her husband-to-be. Finding no sign of life within, she ventured back outside to search the grounds. She walked up the hillside, breathing in deeply to enjoy the crisp Irish air. She loved the scents of nature and inhaled as many as she could on her daily stroll.

Since the ancient and sacred oak tree had given her the mysterious druid magic, all of her senses and physical abilities were enhanced. She could take leaps and bounds on a long morning run without breaking a sweat, and she was enjoying the increase of endurance. Whereas before her power had been dormant, slowly revealing itself just after she met Bowen, now it was fully released. She could feel the power pulsing through her veins. Her body was different—her body somehow *was* her magic, and it possessed too many magical secrets to have learned in one year. Her fire power, the unpredictable and instinctual fighting ability that took over when needed, was still mysterious as ever, even though it had become entirely part of her. She was always learning another layer and seeing yet another shade of herself as life went on.

As she neared the millenia-old stone ruins, she again breathed deeply and reveled in the bright sun blanketing her face and spreading through her hair from root to tip. After the revitalizing energy had soared through her, she walked more comfortably out of the thicket of shrubs at the end of the path and across the now level ground.

"I thought you and Mary were finishing up your wedding dress," Bowen said, eyeing her intently. He was leaning casually against a tree just ahead.

Catherine grinned. "We finished. Why didn't you wait so I could walk with you?"

Bowen shrugged, and his dark brown curls bounced lightly

over his forehead. "I figured you'd be a while. From what I could tell outside the room, you two seemed wrapped up in it."

She swiveled and rested her back against the tree beside him. "I literally was wrapped up in it. It looks beautiful, Bowen. I can't wait for you to see it."

"Anything you wear will look stunning," he said and flashed the charming smile that always made Catherine melt. The intense vibes which seemed to constantly be pulsating off of him caught inside her and surged like nothing she'd ever imagined before she knew him. Her attraction to him was always too strong for her to ignore, and it had grown to the point that standing nearby without the slightest touch was practically torture.

"I think you flatter me too much." She returned the smile, drawing close.

Bowen laughed. "I'm not. It's true."

Gazing into his piercing green eyes, both flecked with glorious gold highlighted from the sun, Catherine leaned her chin against his chest while he enveloped her in his arms. "Are you happy?" she asked.

"Very."

"Only very?"

"Completely."

Catherine closed her eyes, savoring their embrace.

"When are Danny and Bella arriving?" Bowen asked, his voice slightly muffled from her hair.

"Bella said they would show up sometime today. Depending on how fast she could get Danny out of the flat." She snickered. Bowen's chest rumbled with a deep chuckle. "I'm glad he's been staying with her and not who-knows-where."

Bowen nodded, and Catherine opened her eyes. She could feel his fingers running through the ends of her hair, which fell in long, thick waves past her lower back. They smiled at each other, lost in the warmth between them.

Catherine had spent the year relishing her love for Bowen.

After the demise of their mutual enemy, Conall, and his army of loyal followers, she had finally begun to heal. Recasting the druid curse had been meant to trap Conall and his followers back in their caves. Had she succeeded, it would have also locked Bowen once again to the curse's unique role set just for him, after he'd already served for millennia. It would have condemned him to an empty, ageless, and trapped existence. The fear of losing Bowen to that or death itself had disappeared with Conall's defeat, giving Bowen back a normal life, free to age again, free to stay with her.

He wasn't the only one with battle scars. She'd lost her twin sister, Kathleen, at the hands of Conall. This wrong would never be righted, but the peace of knowing justice, and the love of a different kind of soulmate, had given her life meaning again. Catherine had never believed twins could have soulmates other than each other until now. Bowen filled her heart, and they would spend their renewed life together.

He gently squeezed her hand, and instantly Catherine's thoughts returned to the present. The touch was so warm and so perfect, and she never wanted him to let go.

The wedding was the next day, and everything was falling into place. They had always planned to be married, and Bowen had set everything officially in motion during a starlit stroll through the ruins one night when he asked Catherine to set a date. Catherine had wondered what kind of wedding they would have since only a few people knew she was alive. No one in her family but Danny knew. Another loss due to Conall's actions, though this specifically wasn't much of one. She and her siblings were never close to any living relatives other than each other, and none of her connections from her old life through work at the museum—or anywhere else, for that matter—knew either. No one except for Bella, her Australian-born best friend. Since their chance meeting when Catherine first moved to Ireland, their friendship had grown strong; they had become like sisters. Now, in the small village Catherine called home, she had come to depend on Mary, the elderly Irish woman who had taken her and Bowen in as family.

A ripple swept up Catherine's back, as though a bone-cold finger had swiped the length of her spine. She snapped her head around. All she saw was the green grass speckled with ancient stone ruins of various sizes, many of which hovered well above Bowen's tall figure. Looking forward again, she saw the black fae forest, far enough away that she didn't have to worry about a surprise visit but still close enough to summon goosebumps on her arms. Catherine shivered at the memory of her venture inside. The fae she'd met was one of many kinds that existed in the faerie realm, but it was the unknown of each, and their magic, that kept her away.

Catherine watched the sun try to palm the top of the black forest and fail miserably. A hazy black aura remained. The tingling feeling she always got when something ominous was in the air was now moving across her forearms, and she hurriedly rubbed her hands over them.

"Something wrong?" Bowen's voice brought her out of her hyper-focused state and back to the green eyes held steadily on hers. The brows just above them were furrowed.

Casting the bad vibes aside, she shook her head, smiling.

"Nervous about tomorrow?" he asked.

"Not really. I would be if more people were coming."

"You're not in the least bit nervous about the oathing stone?"

"Should I be?" Catherine frowned. "Mary said it's merely tradition."

"It may be considered a symbolic ritual now, but believe me, it's one that's tied to us. Not only is it tied to our vows but our very bodies as well." Bowen shrugged lightly. "I only thought that because you've never seen it before, you might be nervous. Or rather you may be nervous about doing it correctly."

"Maybe a little, now that you say that, but I've known about it for years." Catherine recalled the first time she read about the oathing stone during her studies of Celtic archaeology. She'd learned more when reading myths and legends of the Emerald Isle for pleasure. The oathing stone was an ancient Celtic wedding tradition. According to legend, the stone transferred the wedding oaths to nature, forming a bridge between the sacred site, the couple, and their ancestors. Bowen clearly took it more seriously than she'd thought. "So, what do you want to use as ours?"

"Any piece of wood or stone will do."

Catherine pulled away from his warmth just enough to start walking. "Come on," she said, taking his hand. "Let's pick it out now then."

Bowen chuckled quietly and ran his free hand through the thick curls that covered his head. "It doesn't have to look a certain way."

"Yeah, but I don't want it to be random. This is our special day, for our special traditions. I want our oathing stone to be the best-looking stone or plank of wood I can find."

Walking through the ruins and back down the shrub-lined dirt path on their lover's search, both were so engrossed in their happiness that neither noticed the small white lights flashing far behind them, within the black forest.

A fair, elegant hand slithered across a tree trunk in the middle of a dark wood, the rough bark a drastic contrast to the delicate skin. Its owner followed, stepping out from behind the tree. Small beams of light reflected in the eyes of the beautiful, masculine face. Moving to take another step, he felt a strong tug on the long black braid running down his back. Alarm shot through him as he turned to face his attacker only to find darkness. Relief struck. His braid had caught on the tree's jutting bark. He chuckled to himself and freed his hair. Turning back around, he remained in shadow and waited. Voices were drawing near, and he strained his elongated, sharp-tipped ears to hear them. Two male voices. He recognized them right away.

"I don't trust Cadeyrn," Loïc said.

Judicaël sighed loudly. "He's always been a noble and good ruler."

"Surely you know he reveals nothing of his daily actions as the rest of us do."

"Those are his own affairs."

"Yes, but each king is legally obligated to keep his affairs open." Loïc sounded exasperated, as though struggling to maintain a respectful tone.

"To me." From where Bricius was eavesdropping, he saw Judicaël stop abruptly.

Loïc followed suit and addressed the fae next to him. "My king?"

"Each king is legally obligated to keep his affairs open to me only, as high king. He is not required to have any dealings with you other than what I say. Just as you aren't with him."

Bricius trembled at the steely smoothness in Judicaël's voice. The high king of the fae was as powerful as he was ancient. For everyone's safety, it was important to never tempt his hand.

Loïc bowed. "Yes, my king. Forgive me."

"It is forgiven." Judicaël's right eyebrow twitched, as though a thought had suddenly occurred. "Why do you suspect Cadeyrn? Nothing ill was seen?"

Loïc flinched.

"Out with it!"

The fae stood straighter to look into his king's steel-gray eyes. "He has a lock!"

Judicaël breathed in sharply. Turning away from Loïc, he brought his slender, pale hand out from the folds of his weightless, silky garment and up to his cheek. His garments were nothing short of royal, each a varied pastel color, with plated armor covering his chest and over the front of his legs. Despite the darkness of the forest, where only low, natural fae light emanated, even a mere human would be able to see the high king's beauty. The white light originated from Judicaël's straight, flowing hair, which trailed behind him. It never dirtied or caught on forest debris. Each youthful strand was a crisp white, the envy of every fae creature, even those who were not of their order. The fae kingdoms were vast, but some orders held the form resembling that of mortal humans. Some found it repulsive that their mystical bodies matched those of such barbaric beings, while others found it enchanting and were allured by each human they spotted.

Judicaël came out of his thoughts and lowered his gaze. His high cheekbones and angular face made it difficult for Bricius to see his eyes and decipher any feelings from where he hid. Judicaël was usually easy to read, his every feeling was open for all to see in his mannerisms and expressions. "You know what this means, don't you, Loïc?" he said, exhaling softly.

Loïc nodded.

"Did you see the girl?"

"No, my king. My sources say it was a woman."

"This is deliberately against my wishes, and that of other court orders." Judicaël sighed, his brows knitted together in deep concern.

"Is it not treason against your crown?" said Loïc, his voice filled with passion. "Treason against us all?"

Judicaël's face looked strained as he rubbed a small patch of skin below his right eye. He lowered his voice. "Speak of this to no one. I will deal with it in my own way."

Loïc bowed lower than before to his commanding king, an outstretched arm angled behind him in a customary show of complete obedience and submission, rather than just a bow of acknowledgment.

Judicaël's gaze remained momentarily on his subject's slicked-back hair. The onyx strands glistened and reflected the fae light he cast above Loïc. "Now, leave me and attend to your own," he said with a wave of his hand before slowly walking away.

Bricius watched as his king, King Loïc, quickly rose upright and obeyed. While walking by, Loïc briefly turned his head toward him. Though Loïc's own fae light wasn't as bright as Judicaël's, he still held an angelic glow that spread as far as two steps from him in every direction. Bricius felt comfortable in the darkness, and his fae eyes didn't need the ancient royal light. He could see through every shade of black. Instead of looking noble and loyal, Loïc now looked arrogant and devious. He smiled smugly, and Bricius nodded in acknowledgment before Loïc continued walking.

One step of his mission had been completed. He had succeeded in pleasing his king. Bricius slithered back into the night to return to King Cadeyrn's lands before his absence was noted.

2

A YELLOW CAR pulled up on the gravel road and parked right in front of the cottage. Catherine had been relaxing on the couch for the last hour with Bowen, lazily observing out of the window directly facing the road. As recognition hit, she could feel giddiness rising inside of her, and with a wide smile she unlatched herself from her beloved and ran outside to meet the visitors. Danny climbed out of the passenger side first and stood up just in time to catch her in a full-body hug.

"Hey!" He coughed and sucked in air. "Can you stop slamming into me every time I visit, huh?"

With a final squeeze, Catherine pulled back and released him. "Sorry," she said with a laugh. "I'm just so glad you're here." She heard Bowen walk up behind them, and while Danny heartily greeted him, she turned to Bella, who was stepping out of the car.

"Cathy!"

With small, quick steps, they hurried to the front of the car and met in a springing hug.

"Thank you for coming!" Catherine briefly got a mouthful of

the burgundy scarf billowing around Bella's neck, just as her friend's untamed curls covered her eyes. "It's been too long."

"I missed you too, sweetie!" Bella pulled away, and Catherine could see again. "Tomorrow's your special day. I would have driven for months to see it," she said, smiling. Her brown eyes twinkled as she spoke, and the sun bounced off her blonde, curly locks, creating a glow around the edges.

"Aw, that's grand. Come in," Catherine said, hooking her arm into Bella's and slowly leading the way. "How was the drive? Boring?"

"It was a beaut, don't you worry."

Catherine leaned in closer. "Danny get any part-time work yet?"

"Afraid not," Bella said, her voice slightly strained. "Can we talk about your wedding instead?"

Catherine frowned playfully. Danny hadn't been exactly stable, even before their lives were changed forever last year, but she couldn't hold it against him. Not really. There wasn't much he could do as far as work went, not while he was still considered a missing or dead man to the world. Out there, he didn't have the luxury of someone like Mary who knew their secrets and discreetly gave both Catherine and Bowen jobs in her shops. Danny didn't want to stay in a rural town with them, and Catherine knew he was being extra cautious in order to let her remain hidden away with Bowen. Still, she hoped he wasn't being a pest to Bella.

"Is my brother that much of a handful?"

"Dan is the laziest bloke I've ever seen."

"I can hear you." Danny came up behind them with his and Bella's bags in tow.

"I know, I raised my voice for your benefit," Bella replied, looking over her shoulder with a smirk.

"C'mon, rude much?" His voice had an annoyed tone, but his lopsided smile gave him away.

Shaking out her curls, Bella turned back, walking in step with Catherine. "No, that one's rather lazy, but it's been nice having someone there when I get home from work. He's like a giant pet who doesn't show any affection."

"Hey, I'm nice to you. I ordered the pizza yesterday, didn't I?"

"With my money, Dan."

His lower lip stuck out slightly in a sulky pout. "I would have paid if I could."

They had reached the cottage and walked through the furniture-crowded living room to the old-fashion kitchen with the added warmth of a wood burning stove. Catherine and Bella sat down at the small table after greeting Mary, who was making some eggs. Danny followed Bowen to the guest room to drop off the bags.

"He's been bothering me a lot more lately. He won't leave me alone," Bella was saying as the guys returned. "I don't know what more I can do to make it clear. The guy just doesn't get how crazy he's acting." She smiled at them and sipped her cup of hot tea.

"Who?" Bowen asked.

"Bella's ex," Catherine answered. She wished she'd met the guy, especially when Bella was actually dating him. She felt cheated out of her right to scare him into treating her best friend with respect. Hearing Bella express how many headaches he'd caused her made Catherine want to take over the situation herself, just to make sure it stopped. She could see Bella was more stressed about it than she let on.

Danny sat down in the other free chair at the table. "Yeah, I've never seen the guy, but she's always complaining about him."

Catherine ran her hands through her hair and furrowed her brow. "You told him to stop all contact. It's plain harassment. He sounds dangerous, borderline if not."

"He seems pathetic to me," Danny interjected.

"Even so, I can hardly continue on like this, can I?" Bella sighed. "I tried simply ignoring him too. Nothing works. He's always texting or calling if I take too long to answer him, and he often shows up when I'm out running errands. Other than that, he stalks me on social media. It's really disgusting."

"Has he been to your flat since you broke up?"

"Yes, but not since Dan's been there."

Catherine gripped some of the fabric of her shirt, harshly rubbing it between her fingertips. "You should really alert the Gardaí. Maybe they can talk to him. This has been going on for a year, and it needs to stop."

"I know," Bella said, lowering her gaze. "It's ridiculous, Cathy. I was planning to, and I will after I get back. Anyway, let's not talk about it anymore. I want to hear all about your plans for tomorrow." Bella turned to Bowen, who was leaning against the doorframe to the living room. "Are you wearing a tuxedo or a suit?"

In her excitement at the mention of the wedding, Catherine cut in. "I'll show it to you, and then you can see my dress—oh, did you bring it back with you, Mary?"

"It's in your room," she said, looking up from a pile of peeled potatoes on the kitchen counter. Danny got up from his seat and kindly offered to help peel the rest. Mary happily handed over her vegetable peeler, and he got started.

"Thanks!" Catherine stood and went over to kiss Mary on the cheek before grabbing Bowen's hand to squeeze.

Mary shuffled around the stove to another counter. "Here, old man, help me cut these tomatoes and peppers." She gestured him over with one in each hand. "You're going to be a married man, you need to help out in the kitchen."

Bowen grinned. "Aye." Amusement was still in his eyes when Catherine exchanged a silent endearing look with him, and he started chopping just before she left the room with Bella.

Bella sat in the backseat of her car, feet on the gravel outside, lightly tapping her fingers against the top of her thighs. She scraped the bottoms of her shoes against the stones, enjoying the light drizzle of rain. It didn't matter that her legs were getting damp. In fact, the cold droplets were helping to distract her from the worries that creased her forehead and set her teeth tightly together behind pursed lips.

She took a deep breath and puffed up her cheeks before noisily exhaling. It didn't make her feel much better. Even if she kept her cheery-face on while she told him, she knew Dan wouldn't take her news well. Every time she thought about it the pull of regret made her frazzled, but the wheels had already been set in motion for a few weeks now. She really needed to relax. Even a fraction less stress would give her the boost she needed, but a walk hadn't done the trick. Luckily, she'd escaped to her car just before the downpour began. The beating the rain gave the roof and windows had been brutal, but a pleasant distraction. As it quieted, her feelings reared up even more forcefully.

"Fine," she said aloud, getting out of the car. "I'll get it over with. He can't hate me too much."

Slamming the car door shut, Bella suddenly caught sight of movement just across the way. She choked on a yelp when she saw a beautiful male face staring back at her. He emerged from the drooping shrubs, and her breath hitched. He was tall, and his figure was strange in a way she couldn't put her finger on.

"Bella!" Cathy called through an open window inside the house, but neither Bella nor the newcomer flinched.

Then he smiled. Alarm shot through her, yet she was fascinated. His smile pulled her in, and she forgot her name. The world became devoid of everything except this face and the velvety black hair that framed it. A sinking feeling tunneled down her stomach.

"Bella!"

Cathy's voice. With incredible effort, Bella tore her gaze away to focus on the cottage. Life moved around her once again. "I'm coming!"

She hurried up to the cottage. Placing her hand on the cold, wet doorknob, she felt compelled to look back. A shiver ran up her legs and through her arms. Whatever she'd imagined was nowhere to be seen.

Half-dressed, Danny was standing over his bed while reading —well, more like struggling—through one of Mary's dusty old books. The room was filled with them, all chaotically stacked both on surrounding shelves and windowsills. Parallel to his fold-out bed was a wide, wooden table in the middle of the small library that was also piled with books and covered with dust, only a few of which were in English. *True love. Earth magic.* He turned past several pages.

"True love," he mumbled. A little over a year ago he would have laughed at those words, but after seeing it bloom for real between two very real people, the humor was gone. He skimmed down one page, trying to move past the unpleasant parts about faeries capturing women. He wanted to find out more about magic. Since Catherine was practically made of magic now, he was curious as to how it worked, at least for her.

The floorboards suddenly groaned outside the bedroom door, which he'd left slightly ajar. "Are you decent?" Bella's voice rang through the doorway.

"Not particularly, but I'm wearing pants if that's what you're asking."

Bella gave a breathy snort in reply and pushed past the door into the drafty, dust-filled room. Danny tossed the book back onto the old table and turned around to see her glance from the bed, where he'd strewn all the items from his duffle bag, to his half-naked figure. He greeted her with the lopsided smile that charmed most women at first sight. Danny knew Bella was not most women.

"Sorry, I was changing," he said. He picked up a wrinkled blue dress shirt from the bed and slowly pulled his arms through.

Bella casually shook her head.

"If you wanted to see me dress all you had to do was ask." He smirked. "I'd want to give my best."

Bella rolled her eyes. "Nothing I haven't seen before," she said, flicking her hand.

"What?" He dropped his jaw.

"We've lived together for six months. You're not exactly modest."

Though that was true, Bella didn't seem to mind having him around, despite her verbal outbursts over his apparent laziness. Admittedly, he had spent the last six months lying on her couch. "Did you come in here to complain about me?" he grumbled.

Bella smiled as she plopped herself on top of his empty duffle bag. "I came in here to say you can't come back with me."

Taken aback slightly, he stumbled over his thoughts, trying to organize them. Danny didn't want to think about this right now. How could she say that so easily? Bella had originally been only Catherine's friend, but ever since she let him stay with her as a favor, she'd become his as well. A friend he couldn't imagine being away from now. Not being around her every day . . .

"Why didn't you say so before?"

"I wanted to wait."

He held her gaze. She added, "I'm not happy about it, Dan."

"Then why are you still smiling?"

Her smile vanished, and her eyes narrowed. "I was just being polite." She sighed as she stood up and walked toward the door.

Their playful banter was always fun, but he didn't want a real fight, especially if he might not have enough time to make things between them right again before she went back to Dublin. "Wait," Danny said, reaching out. "I'll deal with it. I'm sorry, I know I can't stay at your flat forever."

The small flame in her eyes died out just as quick as it had flared up, and she stopped at the threshold. She leaned against the door and looked up at him. "It's not that you can't stay with me anymore because you're lazy. I'm subletting my flat while I'm gone."

"Gone? Where are you going?"

She rhythmically tapped her fingers against the doorframe. "Back home to Australia for a stay."

"Why now?" Danny felt his lips quivering slightly and restrained a frown before setting them into a firm line.

"It's only a long holiday. I thought about going to surprise my parents." She paused. "You don't need to give me that twitchy look. I have my Irish citizenship now. This is my home, and I'll be back."

Though he knew her words were meant to reassure him, they didn't. He felt no comfort. He wanted to keep seeing her eyes bright and cheery and keep hearing her voice sweet and bubbly, so he simply nodded.

Bella shrugged slightly and grinned.

Danny did up the last button on his shirt. "How do I look?"

"It's bodgy. You don't have any other dress shirts?"

"No, they were all literally burned up. Someone gave me this out of pity when I was staying on their couch." He winked.

Jumping from couch to couch, week to week, while staying with strangers at first, had been tiring. At the time he hadn't known what else to do. Living with Bella had given him a chance to relax, to grieve, really. Little had he known that quitting his job last year and moving to Ireland to live with his sister would be just the beginning of things toppling over for him—the beginning of a giant, horrifying snowball rolling down a mountain, gaining momentum. Now he was still faced with his original question: what was he going to do with his life?

"Right, I remember. Are you almost ready to face the world again?" she asked, staring him down.

Danny shifted his weight, uncomfortable. "I can't really do anything since I'm a dead man."

"I'm sure we can figure out a way for you to come forward and say you're fine without snitching on Catherine. There has to be something we haven't thought of."

"Not a chance. It's a risk I don't want to take. She's the only sister I have left, and I want her to be happy. On the other hand, where my life is going, I still can't say I know yet."

"Unless you want to live here forever or move around on strangers' couches the rest of your life, I think you need to decide sooner rather than later." Bella straightened up and folded her arms across her chest. "Maybe you can do something with those wild, outdoor sports. I remember how much you liked them. You used to be such a thrill junkie when I met you, and now you never go outside unless you have to. Your body is too athletic to just waste away. Freshen up those muscles." Her playful voice filled his ears and made him feel warm.

"Is that your way of saying I'm attractive?" He wiggled his eyebrows.

Bella laughed. "Sure."

He smirked for a second before looking down and examining his shirt.

"Come here." She moved toward him and raised her soft, feminine hands to his collar, running them along the edges and then down the entirety of the shirt, trying to decrease the wrinkles.

Standing this close to her, he could smell her strawberry-scented body spray, made more potent by her strawberry-scented hair. He took a moment to breathe it in, and almost instantly felt himself overheating. The tops of her fingers grazed his neck, leaving small trails of goosebumps. He cleared his throat and leveled his gaze, trying to catch hers. "So you wouldn't say it that way?"

She briefly glanced at his face before continuing her task. "No, I wouldn't. I flirt, but I don't like to play weird games."

"How would you want someone to say you're attractive, then?"

"I prefer a more direct method."

Danny widened his eyes. "Really? You want some guy to be obnoxiously blunt as hell?"

"Don't be daft."

"Then what do you mean? Be like that obsessive ex of yours?"

"No, of course not," she said, her voice lowering slightly. "I just mean flirting's fun, but after it, I'd rather you get to the point and say what you mean."

He wasn't sure he could bring himself to be that direct with her. He'd always been able to tell a woman what was on his mind; dating used to hold most of his attention, next to sports, until last year. After all, flirting with every girl in sight had always been second nature. He felt something different around Bella, something real, and that made him second guess all of his old lines until he was forced to a standstill, stuck at the flirting stage. After a moment's silence, Danny cleared his throat again. "I like flirting with you."

"That's a good example." She grinned and gave a small laugh. "There," she announced, resting her arms on top of his shoulders. Her face inched closer than normal, and he felt his pulse race. "That's the best I can do without steam or an iron. I'm sure they have one though." Her arms slipped off. "I'll go ask—"

"No," he croaked. Danny took a second to swallow back the frog. "Don't bother them with it. It looks good, thanks. The ceremony's outside at dusk anyway." He couldn't help but smile at her large, inquiring eyes.

"True enough." The scent of strawberry lingered as Bella looped her arm through his and pulled him out the door. "I like flirting with you too."

3

CATHERINE STOOD in front of the bathroom mirror and stared into her large, hazel eyes before scanning every inch of her reflection for any sign of imperfection. Behind her half-bare shoulders, her deep red hair flowed down the back of her gown. The lace at the top of the dress formed a V-neck, which dipped into and layered over the silky satin fitted closely against her torso. She feared a single deep breath would pop the cloth-covered buttons lining the back of it. The long sleeves covered her goosebumps, but outwardly, even in her emotionally heated state, she looked cool and breezy. All she had to do was think of Bowen, and she would be fine.

Mary popped her head in. "My girl, it's nearly dusk. You ready?"

Catherine could hardly believe how fast the day had gone, or how long it had taken for this day to even arrive. Finally, she would marry the loveliest and kindest soul she'd ever known. She only hoped all of the effort she made in looking beautiful today would take Bowen's breath away out there. After one more mirror scan, she turned and nodded.

Mary looked as though she held back a sob or two. "Good gracious you look lovely."

Catherine breathed out in relief. "Thank you, Mary." She reached over to squeeze her hand, and in the moment, they exchanged an affectionate smile. Mary was another wonderful light that had entered her life after darkness had crept there, and Catherine felt a special happiness in her heart that she could share this day with her. "Help me out?" Picking up the end of the train, Mary hurried into the tiny bathroom to gather the rest.

In such a gown, the trek to the ceremony took longer than usual, but with rising anticipation and the feel of the cold soil under her bare feet, Catherine enjoyed each step. With Mary in tow, she walked over the hill and found four souls eagerly awaiting her by the remains of the ancient oak. As she passed through the shadows of the large ruin's stones, she released some of her magic, and her steps lit up the path with a yellow glow that resonated throughout the entire area. Bella gasped and slapped her hands over her mouth. No one else reacted other than with silent awe. The more level ground aided her, and Catherine reached the others in no time. Her heart raced when Bowen, clad in a charming black suit and tie, took her hands and smiled. Warmth spread through her as she smiled back, and all of her nerves vanished.

The sixth person in the small group was the officiant, Pastor Kelley. Catherine knew the kind, elderly minister from town. He was often in the bookshop where she worked under Mary's instruction, and she'd held many a conversation with him. He always expressed his views openly, believing that there was more to the world than mortals knew and that other worlds existed too. As such, Mary and Pastor Kelley were old friends. Being so open-minded, he had agreed to discreetly officiate.

Pastor Kelley stood to her left as she faced Bowen's loving gaze. After reading from The Good Book, he looked up with a fatherly smile. "Who has the stone?"

Danny stepped forward and offered up the hand-sized object.

"Thank you. Now Bowen, lay your hands on the stone."

Bowen let go of Catherine and did so. Then he looked into her eyes. "What I say now, I say in the presence of God, and all my ancestors, both living and dead. I ask them to witness my oath to the woman I love, by the vows I bring forward."

"Catherine." Kelley nodded.

Being put on the spot to speak made her slightly nervous again, but when she placed her hands on top of Bowen's, carefully maneuvering her fingers to touch the smooth surface of the stone, she refocused and relaxed into him. Her words flowed easily together as she repeated what Bowen had said, and when she finished, the minister cued Bowen with a look.

Bowen smiled at her again, and in the glowing light radiating from the ground beneath them and the stars above them, she thought she saw a hint of a glaze in his eyes. "I'm filled with you, Catherine, from the surface of my skin to the bottom of the deep pool my soul resides in. You are all of me, and for a lifetime and beyond I belong to you." If the glow around them were coming from candles and not her power, the longing in his deep voice would have melted them all.

Catherine swallowed, hoping her voice wouldn't falter. "Bowen, I will always fight with you and for you, because you are my best friend and my love. With every breath I take, I love you more, and when the day comes that I stop breathing, the universe will still see my love for you expanding."

Bella sobbed lightly behind her. Catherine and Bowen shared a small grin. Bella was always so emotional.

Pastor Kelley removed the stone from under their hands and placed it on the grass in front of the old stump of the great oak tree directly behind him. He stepped forward again and continued. "Bowen, do you take Catherine Green to be your wife?"

"I do." The mixture of his rich voice and those two little words sent sparks flying in Catherine's stomach.

"Catherine, do you take Bowen, of the ancient druids, to be your husband?"

The sparks burned upward to her beating heart and dissolved into her lifeblood. "I forever do."

"Now you may place your rings as a daily symbol of your commitment," he said. They each took one band of white gold out of Bella's palm and slid them on each other's ring fingers. "Under God, this starry sky, and these rolling hills, I'm pleased to pronounce you both as one. You may seal your union with a kiss."

Catherine felt Bowen wrap around her like a blanket, and she fell into a kiss she never wanted to end. When it did, she opened her eyes to see stars framing his curly hair and her fire-glow reflected in his smiling green eyes. It seemed as though she had awakened into a dream. Bowen kissed her again, and she wanted to stay forever in this perfect dream.

The sound of clapping eventually broke through in the foggy distance and brought them out of their loving trance. Danny and Bella crowded around, hugging and congratulating them, while Mary hung back until she could get in her own congratulatory hugs without an elbow fight.

"Thank you." Catherine couldn't stop smiling as she hugged her arms around each of them tightly. "Thank you for being here and for everything," she said as warm tears bubbled at the corners of her eyes. "I love you all."

"Don't waste your time thanking me. Be off to the dinner I prepared back at the cottage," said Mary before leaning in. "I made up your room," she whispered. "And since I share a bedroom wall with you, I'll be staying elsewhere for tonight."

Startled, Catherine pulled back and blushed deeply. She nodded and smiled with gratitude.

Bowen swooped in, grabbed her by the waist and pulled her to him. Everyone else was preoccupied with their own lively conversations. "The stone," he said quietly in her ear and gestured over to where the oathing stone rested.

“It’s supposed to be given off to nature, isn’t it?” She leaned in to kiss him again. “I think that’s the perfect spot.”

One corner of Bowen’s lips perked up. “Let’s go eat that dinner.”

When the dinner of jest and fellowship was over, Pastor Kelley left, and Mary went outside to enjoy the night sky, as she often did. Danny and Bella cleaned the kitchen. Catherine smiled as her groom took her by the hand and led her to their room.

Colorful flower petals decorated the bedroom floor. She kicked them up, and they blew around her, falling on her dragging gown and slipping between her toes. Mary had replaced the regular bedding with a fluffy-soft white set. Catherine cooed when she ran her hands along the foot of the bed.

“Almost makes me not want to sleep in it,” Bowen said with a laugh, trailing his own hand along it.

“Really?” Catherine stood up straighter, a smirk on her face.

“Almost,” he repeated, pulling her close and running his hands down her back.

Catherine woke to the delightful singsong of chirping coming through the open window behind her. A cool breeze gently brushed her skin, which contrasted the feel of the sun warming her back. She watched its rays dance on the wall’s gray wooden panels. They mingled with the shadows of the white lace window curtains, blowing in delicate waves. It reminded her of a jellyfish, and Catherine’s lips curved into a small smile at the sight.

The old analog alarm clock, strategically placed on the dresser across the room, quietly ticked away as Catherine lay in the crisp white sheets she shared with the handsome man next to her. She turned around to face him and the sun. He was still sleeping soundly. Catherine loved seeing him relaxed, and watching the curve of his mouth twitch every so often as he dreamed. She gently ran her fingers through his brown curls. She'd always felt a need to do this, never quite getting her fill every time she did. Catherine hadn't shared this fact with Bowen yet, but whenever she did it while he was awake, he would give her a knowing look. She ran her eyes over the length of his naked body, drinking in every inch.

Suddenly the alarm rang loudly. Catherine jumped up and ran to end its tirade with a slap, cursing herself for forgetting to turn it off.

"Sorry, I thought about that last night, but I forgot," Bowen said, his voice groggy.

"You were distracted," she added, grinning to herself.

After mentally shooting the clock with invisible darts, Catherine turned around to see Bowen's bright eyes and charming smile. Though she was comfortable with him, she quickly remembered she was naked and felt mildly awkward just standing there. She smirked when she noticed Bowen taking in the view with apparent enjoyment. She leaped back onto the bed, and he rose to meet her in an embrace. They fell into the pillowy mass below them, quietly chuckling. Catherine placed her hand on the soft, warm skin of his chest, and then pressed her cheek against it. She reveled in this feeling of belonging, of happiness. She wanted to stay here forever. Forever happy.

A chill suddenly ran up her spine, and she shivered.

"You're not cold, are you?" Bowen sounded surprised but didn't stop tracing a pattern on her back with one caressing finger.

"No, just a shiver," Catherine replied, shifting slightly to look up at him so their noses were touching. "Are you happy?"

Bowen's eyebrows furrowed. "Of course. You keep asking me that. Isn't it obvious?"

"Yeah, but I mean . . . truly happy? Nothing could get to you now?"

"I am truly happy, Catherine. As long as I have you, I can get through everything else."

Catherine smiled. "That's what I thought you'd say."

Bowen looked at her lovingly. "And you?"

She nodded. "Me too."

Bowen leaned in, kissing her mouth first then moving to her cheeks and down behind her ear. He burrowed his face roughly in her hair and neck and breathed in deeply. She knew he loved the peaches-and-cream lotion she wore. Catherine relished each moment he spent exploring every inch of her, and she sighed heavily in pleasure.

"Love me?" she whispered in his ear.

"I do."

"Want me?"

"I do," he rasped.

"Have me."

Draped lazily across the bed, Catherine watched the flower petals flutter in the occasional breeze coming through the window. Absentmindedly, she happily kicked her legs behind her, even as Bowen grabbed her calves and planted kisses on her skin.

She gasped. "Ouch!" She looked back and saw blood running down her lifted leg.

"What happened?" Bowen asked, wide-eyed.

She sat up quickly to examine the wound on her ankle. "I don't know. It's bleeding, but there isn't any opening that I can see." She stretched across the bed to get her robe. "I'm just going to go clean it off."

Bowen carefully took her ankle in his hands but suddenly dropped it like a brick before he fell and rolled over himself, pinning her bloody leg under him.

"Bowen?" Catherine said, managing to slide her leg out. Wild with worry, all she could focus on was the sound of her husband's muffled agony. Her heart was encircled and gripped by something sharp, and she felt it burrowing the beginnings of a deep empty black hole. "Are you all right?" She grasped his shoulders and shook him. He was shivering under her hands.

"I'm so cold, so very tired," he said, his voice strained.

She quickly covered him with a sheet. "Lie back." She struggled to help him into a reclined position and then secured the comforter around him as best she could.

Catching sight of his face, she recoiled. His skin was a ghostly gray, and there was no color in his lips. "Bowen!" He didn't open his eyes. She said his name again and again, each time more forcefully, but still his eyes remained closed. Frantic but afraid to leave him, Catherine shouted for help. Danny ran in first, followed by Bella.

"My God, what's wrong with him?" Danny asked.

"I—I don't know!" Catherine said, unable to keep the desperation out of her voice. "He's sick or something. He won't answer me. I don't know if he can hear me." She looked down at his face again. "Bowen!"

Bella wrung her hands at the door. "Don't panic, Cathy, I'm sure—" she broke off. "I'll get Mary."

"Hurry!" Catherine called as Bella dashed out of the room.

Danny moved to the bed and patted her shoulders as she hunched over her husband. Bowen wasn't shaking anymore—in fact, he wasn't moving at all. He looked like a corpse, but he was still breathing, though faintly. Catherine felt that at any second her heart would break inside her chest and that every flying shard would tear through it and finish her. Frozen at his side, she squeezed his limp hand in hers. Then all of a sudden, something changed. Her stomach dropped.

She looked up at Danny and barely heard the words escaping her own lips. "I don't think he's breathing."

4

CATHERINE COULD ONLY HOLD her breath as she watched Danny lean down and put his finger under Bowen's nose. A few seconds later he withdrew his hand and laid it across Bowen's chest. After what seemed like hours, he pulled it away and squeezed her shoulder.

"It's just slowed. He still has a heartbeat."

Exhaling deeply, Catherine relaxed her tight posture only slightly. She didn't have to break apart after all. Not yet. "I can't do this. I almost lost him once. I can't lose him now. Not ever, but especially not now," she said, tears filling her eyes. The fear of losing him was a wound she'd carried for too long. It had become a scar, but now it was open again, and bleeding hot inside of her like the strange blood on her ankle.

"I know," Danny said soothingly. "Come here." He wrapped her in a hug, and she reluctantly conceded.

Pulling out of his embrace, she continued to cry. Danny tugged on her cheeks, just like he'd done when they were children and she would scrape her knee while playing. "Stop it," she said between sobs. "I'm sorry, nothing but him waking up will help me."

Danny blinked a few times. "Sorry," he said softly and gave an awkward shrug. Catherine felt worse that she couldn't even pretend to feel better for her brother's sake. Right now, all she cared about was Bowen.

Suddenly a searing pain shot through the base of her skull, and she heard a woman screaming. The sensation was so blinding that it took her a moment to realize the screams were her own. Danny hovered and shouted over her, but she couldn't tell what he was saying. The pain moved upward as if someone with coal-hot knives for fingers were burning lines into her scalp. Just when she thought she couldn't stand it anymore, the pain stopped. Only a dull ache remained along the sides of her face and behind her ears.

"Catherine?" Danny's shaky voice sounded far away.

Breathing in short, small breaths, Catherine realized she wasn't on the bed anymore but huddled in a ball on the floor. She could feel the hard floorboards beneath her worn body. A cool breeze swooped down from the window, blowing a bunch of flower petals into her face. Catherine slowly opened her eyes and pushed herself up to a sitting position. "Danny." She hardly recognized her hoarse voice.

"I'm here," he said. He was sitting next to her on the floor.

"Are you okay?"

"Me?" He looked at her incredulously. "Yeah, I'm fine. What the hell was that?"

Tentatively, Catherine touched her head. All she could focus on was that nightmarish pain, a perfect addition to this nightmarish morning. "I don't know, but whatever it was is over now, I think."

"Uh, no. You need to look at yourself right now."

"What? Why?"

"Because you have something written on you."

Letting her hand drop as if it were deadweight, she looked blankly at him.

"I'm dead serious. I'll cut my right hand off if I'm lying."

Catherine tried to stand. Wobbling too much, she rested the upper half of her body on the end of the bed. Seeing Bowen's still figure snapped her out of her foggy state. Everything came crashing back down on her. What was happening was inconceivable. *Why?* The word resounded and bombarded everything inside of her. With renewed sorrow, she grabbed her face, and immediately froze, every limb rigid. She could feel something under her fingertips. Panicked, she whirled around and with Danny's aid, managed to make it to the small mirror on her dresser.

It looked like someone had taken a pen and drawn strange black lines on her skin, or rather, burned them into her skin. They ran down the sides of her face and ended just under her jawbone, partly on her neck. Some connected to lines coming from behind her ears. Lifting the back of her hair briefly, she saw that the lines moved up her scalp as well, where she'd felt the mind-bending pain.

"What is this?" she mumbled, horror-stricken.

Danny continued holding her waist to keep her from falling and met her eyes in the mirror. "I know you're really freaked out right now, but before anything else happens, I want to tell you I love you." Only the last three words reached Catherine, the rest of her attention was boiling in turmoil. "I didn't get to say it to Kathleen before she died," he added.

His words briefly flashed her back to that hellish day, watching Kathleen die right in front of her was like having her guts torn out all at once. Catherine had already been through hell and back, and she wasn't going to give up and make it easy for whatever magic was attacking them now. "Me too, Danny." She turned all the way around to face him, pushing her overwhelming panic behind her. "But I'm not going to die like this."

He looked doubtful but then nodded stiffly.

"I mean it," she said, determination filling her. "I'm not. Now, listen to me." She turned and sat on the small ottoman in the corner of the room. "I can handle myself for now. Go help Bella find Mary. I need her." She felt the hot trickle of blood running down her ankle again. Discreetly, she moved her leg adjacent to the ottoman, trying to hide it from Danny.

"Okay, I'm going." He stopped at the threshold. "Are you sure you'll be all right alone?"

"It's just for a few minutes."

"But all it takes is one second!"

"I told you, I'm not dying like this," she said, meeting his eyes with unblinking seriousness. "Go on!"

Danny rushed out, and she was alone with her dying beloved. *That is what's happening, isn't it?* she thought.

No, she couldn't bear to consider it. What was happening to him—to them? Why were both of them being viciously mangled from the inside out? Bowen wasn't magical, he had only been a doctor. He had learned the common knowledge of his ancient people but never practiced the magic himself. Something magical was obviously doing this. Her reopened wound was a red flag. Could it be her magic hurting them? The timing of their intimacy coincided too much to not be connected somehow. Staring at the empty space directly in front of her, she slowly shook her head. No. That theory didn't feel right. She wouldn't contemplate losing Bowen from her own magic. The magic that had only aided and saved both of them before. It was all she could do not to dwell on it.

After grabbing a box of tissues off of the dresser, she set to dabbing the blood away on her ankle with one hand, and gently pulling her falling hair out of her face with the other. She was careful not to tug on her sore scalp. Selfish thoughts repeated over and over in her mind. She couldn't remember her world without Bowen, and she didn't want to. She couldn't go back to that. The oath she'd taken last night was merely a sprinkle on a thoroughly layered cake. Catherine wasn't afraid of dying. If Bowen died first, she would freely jump in after him.

Eventually she took a break from trying to dry it all with the tissues. She stretched out her hand over where the blood seeped out of her ankle and quieted her wildly beating heart long enough to focus on her fire magic. She called to it. It circled from the deep but didn't ignite at her will. Instead, it rolled over itself with a flicker and something in the dark stamped it out of sight. Catherine pulled her shaking hand to her chest. Why couldn't she summon the magic? She couldn't heal her ankle again, let alone the scalp markings which disturbed her even more. *Mary will know what to do, Mary will help,* she told herself, patting her chest. Mary's extensive knowledge of magic passed down to her through the generations would definitely point Catherine in the right direction.

She looked over at Bowen's grayed and weakened figure, the life draining out of him. When they were nearly separated in the past, he'd been saddened but could cope. She wouldn't be able to do that. How could he cope if he loved her as much as she loved him? Catherine shook her head, willing the insecurities away. No, she knew Bowen loved her and would fight to the death to be with her. She was just weak, as always, even with her magic. The magic that was now just as emotionally unstable as she was.

Mary suddenly appeared in the doorway, distraught. "What's the matter? The front door was wide open and there was no one in sight."

"Bella didn't find you?"

Mary shook her head, and her eyes widened when she saw the blood staining the disheveled white bedding.

Catherine couldn't speak and just pointed to Bowen. Mary rushed to his side and began examining him.

"I've never seen this before, Caty," she said after a few moments. "How did it start?"

"It was sudden, no warning." She swallowed hard. "We were

just lying in bed and then he changed color, closed his eyes. He's been that way ever since."

Mary's furrowed brow flinched slightly as she turned to look Catherine over, her clever eyes lingering in particular on the sides of her face. "And you? Something's terribly off as well."

"I don't know anything." She couldn't seem to keep the slight tremble out of her voice. "I'm completely lost." Catherine's foot twitched involuntarily. "Except just before Bowen collapsed, the wound on my ankle started bleeding—only there was no wound."

"The one I made at the shop?"

Catherine nodded. The bleeding had stopped at last after several tissues were thoroughly bloodied. Relieved for that at least, she took off her robe and began getting dressed, choosing clothes randomly: a wide-pleated skirt and bulky Christmas sweater.

"But you healed it with your fire just after, didn't you?" Mary said, continuing to examine Bowen.

Catherine sat back down, but the sweater was already making her feel much too hot. "Yes, before I got home." She rummaged through the open drawer next to her, pulled out a tank top, and quickly changed into it.

"You didn't forget how? No mistake?"

"No, none."

"My dear, something is drawing from both of you, taking your strength. It's unsteady though. I don't know what that means. You should both be dead by now."

Catherine frowned. "How can something take from both of us at the same time?"

"You are one with the old man now. Anything that affects him affects you, and it works both ways."

Catherine blew out a sigh of relief. It wasn't her fault as she'd feared, but then, what was the cause? "So how can I find out which of us is being attacked, and by what?"

"I cannot say, my dear. All I can do is watch over you."

Frustration washed over Catherine. "No, I'm not going to sit here and watch him die! Is there someone who can help me?" She took off the tank top and put on a long-sleeved shirt instead. It would be chillier outside.

"This level of magic is beyond any human, dear."

Floorboards creaked as heavy steps ran across them. Danny appeared at the door and came to a halt. "I couldn't find her," he said hoarsely, out of breath.

"Mary's here now," Catherine replied.

"No, Bella!"

"What? She's not anywhere outside?"

"No, I checked everywhere, even some of the shops down the road. No one's seen her."

"That yellow car is still here," Mary said, looking at Danny and tilting her head thoughtfully. "She didn't drive away, my boy."

Danny gulped in another gallon of air. "I'm telling you, something's wrong. Bella is gone."

Catherine felt his words shoot through her and pin themselves on what was left of her heart. What was happening, and why was it happening all at once? As far as she knew she couldn't do anything about most of it, but she could do something about this. She shot up. Wobbly at first, she quickly recovered and rushed past Danny.

"Where are you going?"

"To find her," she snapped. The idea of Bella being in danger stuck in her skin like thorns. What if her stalker ex-boyfriend had escalated his obsession to the next level? Not letting the fear rise from the pit of her stomach, she focused all of her energy on anger. She needed physical strength to get to her friend.

"I'm sure she's fine, Caty!" she heard Mary call, but it was no use. Catherine was already down the hall and out the door.

Catherine grew increasingly tired as she followed the path that weaved around the cottage, searching the back gardens and any spots that Danny might have missed. Puffing up her cheeks with air in frustration, she tried to think where Bella might have gone to look for Mary first. Catherine moved up the dirt path toward the ruins, panting heavily with each step.

Upon reaching the ancient stones, exposed to the open fields, she felt the winds making dozens of figure eights around them and pushing her this way and that. She winced, her scalp tattoos stinging. Catherine leaned against one of the large, looming stones for stability. A gust blew so hard it took her breath with it as it passed.

"Bella!" she shouted.

All she heard was wind. She continued searching, moving through the rocky maze until she came to the ancient oak tree's remains. Hovering over it, she tried to see its fully bloomed form in her mind, reimagining it as she often did. Something wasn't quite right. *The stone!* The oathing stone was gone. She nearly fell over from the violent flinch of realization. Frantically, she looked around for any sign of another person, but there was no one.

Who could have taken the stone? Why? It was merely a tradition. A harmless, respectful tradition. What unknowing person could have been trespassing here between last night and the present just to take a random rock by an oak stump? It didn't make any sense. She paced ahead a bit, out of reach of the tall ruins and their mild shade.

Holding her breath as another gust of wind rushed past her, she felt her ankle grow hot again. She reached down to try to clean off the blood in the grass but then paused. Under her foot was a torn burgundy scarf. Bella's. Ahead of her, the black forest stood in the distance, sinister as a coming storm.

"Fae," she gasped out.

Taking off at a run, she felt the weight of everything crashing down on her, crushing her, leaving her breathless. Not much time had passed before Catherine fell to her knees and gripped the soft dirt in her hands until all of her fingernails had soil under them. She dropped her head and lay on the ground, planting her face in it. She was so distraught, she barely noticed the harsh twigs and sporadic tufts of grass stabbing and scratching her. *Breathe.* She just needed to breathe normally again.

One breath came, light and shallow, then one more, deep and life-giving. Her lungs retracted and then released a long, steady flow of air. A recent memory surfaced; lying peacefully with Bowen and listening to his deep breathing under her ear. The memory pulled at her aching heart but also filled it up with the only thing left she had to hold on to. Hope. Catherine found her strength again and pushed off toward the black forest.

At the edge of the wood, Catherine hesitated. The familiar blackness made her skin crawl, but the thought of never seeing Bowen again was even more terrifying. "I hate this," she whispered, but she couldn't do anything for Bowen or herself if she didn't know what was wrong. Maybe it was somehow her fault. She couldn't bear it if she hurt him and didn't know it.

Catherine slowly raised her hands to look at her palms. After a moment they began to tremble. She hastily folded them into fists at her sides and swallowed back the anxiety. No. Without finding out how, she couldn't help Bowen yet—but she could save her friend. Even in her weakened state, she would do whatever it took. It was the only starting point she could think of.

One step forward. She stopped again. A hideous screeching

erupted somewhere in the distance. Quickly clasping her ears, she crouched down and scrunched her face, repulsed by the noise. It was a woman's voice behind the tortured wailing. The wind blew more harshly around her until all sound ended at once, leaving her shivering.

Grappling with her balance, Catherine rose and gasped loudly. What if the wail was a warning from Bella's captor? Or had Bella been killed for going into the fae's black forest? Catherine dashed into the blackness, leaving any lingering hesitation behind her. Her life was only meaningful if she kept her loved ones safe. She would plead for the fae's help again, and give them whatever they wanted so long as she could save Bowen and find Bella.

The darkness of the forest slowed her down dramatically, but she pushed through as fast as she could sense the surrounding space. So far nothing seemed the same as her first time in the fae forest, even though she was sure she had entered the same way. It was just as dark, but the footpath wasn't as effortless a trek as before. She kept hitting tree trunks and their protruding branches, stabbing her feet on many a pointed unknowable object, and falling into bushes.

Eventually, she felt her way to a clearer path, and by this time her eyes adjusted enough to quicken her pace. Within a short time, unlike her last visit, the path abruptly turned to the left. The uncanny blackness instantly cleared and revealed a regular forest with normal light. Small animals skittered to and fro, but then something larger darted across the path. Someone. Her eyes were merely human and couldn't register what they were seeing. She planted her feet and waited.

"Come out!" she shouted, growing more agitated by the second. It moved behind the trees, and she could only spot a shadow between a few of them. The sound of the figure's movements ceased briefly. "Show yourself!"

A tall, unearthly-looking woman, dressed in transparent silver garments that hung down past her feet, appeared on the path as if from thin air. Her long raven-black hair was plaited with jeweled silver. Everything about the fae glowed. Her milky skin almost blended into the air around her like a mist, and even her ebony hair was lit up along the edges, smudging out the air around it in blotches, like spilled ink on paper.

"Why are you following me?" Catherine asked flatly.

The fae gave her an icy stare in return, the beautiful violet of her eyes offsetting her obvious disdain only slightly. She didn't answer, so Catherine raised her hands, seemingly in a gesture of peace, though she was really preparing to fight. The silver-clad woman gave her a knowing look.

"I'm not here to do anything but find my friend," Catherine continued. "One of the fae has taken her."

The wind picked up around them as the fae eyed her carefully. "You should not be here, druid woman."

"I've been here once before, through the black forest, and met with one of your people there. I mean no intrusion."

"Those are part of Cadeyrn's lands," she said with a sneer. "What you did there means nothing to me here. You are a disgusting violation." She looked over Catherine as though she were covered in hideous boils.

The wind grew fiercer, and Catherine raised her arm to shield herself from the gravel and twigs flying in every direction. "I just want to find my friend, and I'll leave," she said, raising her voice over the thick air pressing against her ears.

"Begone, and know that any human woman I see will instantly be spat back out where she belongs."

"I can't leave without her, and I won't let you hurt her."

"Begone!" With those words, a billowing silver windstorm spun around the fae's arms, and with a flick of her fingers, she thrust it at Catherine.

5

CATHERINE'S FIRE met the silvery winds just in time. It rushed out of her fingertips in a flash of beaming power so hot it melted the leaves off the nearby trees and charred the grass directly under them to blackened embers. The force of the opposing fae was so great that Catherine, in her weakened state, wasn't sure how long she could fight it.

Her fire blazed in the magic wind. It gave the illusion of superior strength, but the fire never reached her enemy because somehow the fae's magic was shooting it back at her. The silvery wind was like nothing she'd ever imagined. When the wind cut through her fire, it whipped and snapped at her cheeks, her hair, and at any exposed skin. Each painful sting clung to her like lingering perfume, slowly suffocating her. Catherine cursed under her breath with every fresh whipping. Her vision blurred as the wind swiped the water from her eyes. She closed them tight and fell to her knees, arms outstretched and shaking.

The familiar burning on her scalp returned, and the remainder of her concentration disappeared in a flash. She screamed and grabbed at her face before tearing at her hair in fits. With her guard down, her magic stopped. The wind dropped her like a sack of potatoes, but all she knew was the pain.

Blackness carried her to oblivion. Here her soul rested and waited. All too quickly her senses returned, and she found herself staring at dewdrops slowly dripping off faded green and brown grass. Everything smelled clean and damp. Small circles of light sparkled and winked at her from within each drop. In one motion, Catherine sat up. It was morning, and she was alone on the forest floor in the fae's realm. How had she not been killed?

Catherine couldn't contemplate what had happened, and was just thankful she saw no sign of her attacker. Since her magic had returned to her, at least for now, she quickly set to using her fire to heal her ankle once more. She silently hoped that it would keep this time around.

Resting her dirt-covered elbows on her legs, she gently ran her hands through her hair, combing it back out of her face. Pulling her fingers through didn't provide the satisfying feeling it usually did. Instead, a thunderbolt of alarm shot through her as a large clump of hair remained in her palm. She stared down at her hand, and then at the red locks that hung long and flowing over her wrists and falling into a large, wavy mass on her thighs.

Frantically, she ran her fingers through her hair again and found herself holding another clump. She did it again, and again, and again until she sat in a large red nest of her own making. This was not the result of hysteria. Could the magic tattoo have been the cause? *This—this is too much!* Catherine slammed her hands on the dirt in front of her, shut her eyes and counted to ten. Between each number she uttered, she took a long, meditative breath. The breathing calmed her rattled nerves, though tears still slipped through her eyelids and dripped off her chin. When she reached the last number, she opened her eyes to try the world again. Almost afraid to touch it, Catherine slowly rubbed her alarmingly bald head. She traced the curious indented patterns with unsteady fingers.

Catherine quickly looked around, feeling exposed and vulnerable. Whatever these markings were, whatever they meant, she didn't want them visible to prying eyes. She tore a large strip from her skirt, then another from her shirt, revealing more of her skin to the elements. Since her magic came to her last year, she hadn't felt real cold on her skin once, until now. The air was damp with a chill that glazed over her. She couldn't understand what was happening, only that she was weakening and running out of time.

With the help of Bella's torn scarf she'd pocketed, she fashioned the strips of cloth into a head covering and was surprised to find it provided much-needed warmth and security. Enough for her to regain the confidence to move forward. Hesitating a moment, she remembered the deal she'd made with the first faerie she had met, and worriedly eyed the pile of red locks. The fae valued women's hair for reasons they didn't reveal. Without further delay, she set the pile of hair on fire and watched it turn instantly to ash. After double-checking that every strand of hair had been destroyed in the fire, Catherine set off cautiously to find her friend, or a fae who would.

Luminous golden feathers rustled as Loïc strolled through a particularly empty part of his forests, a mostly overgrown, dark space. Though his face was twisted in anxiety, his demeanor was calm, his stride relaxed. His soft glow lit up the shrub-filled dirt beneath his feet. A shadow moved across his path just ahead, and Loïc stopped.

"Come forward, Bricius," he called.

Bricius spun out from the darkness and bowed elaborately, getting down on one knee, one arm across his chest. "Sire."

"Do you have it?"

Bricius whipped his other arm from behind his back and held out his hand, palm face up.

Loïc's eyes grew as he took the proffered item. "And there's no mistake?" His voice was stern.

"None, sire. I watched the ritual for confirmation."

"Was there anything else you took that could prove helpful to me?" Loïc caressed the article in his hands.

The dark-haired spy leaned heavily on his raised knee. Loïc didn't notice the wince that flashed across his subject's face. "None, my king."

Loïc eyed Bricius, brow furrowed. He sensed something not entirely loyal within his stealthy subject playing spy, but looking back to the object in his palm, he knew he had already won what truly mattered. "You may rise."

Bricius stood tall, almost the same height as Loïc. His long braid hung over one shoulder. He clasped his hands behind his back and raised his chin.

"The war has reached another stage in my plans," Loïc said. "This will give me the final advantage to get what I want. Return to Cadeyrn, but be sure to keep up your façade until I say. He mustn't catch a glimpse of your disloyalty, or a whiff that I have this. Not yet."

"You have my word, sire." Bricius disappeared into the black just as a cold breeze blew past.

Loose ringlets of gold blew into the void, and Loïc reached out and caught several between his fingers. They bore a hint of strawberry scent.

Danny was frantic. He rushed from one room to another and then double-checked the grounds. Bella and his sister had vanished. He had to find them. Mary could look after Bowen. Finding his way back to town, he spent over an hour thoroughly checking every shop, and behind every cottage and building, pretending to be as casual as he possibly could. Ultimately, he made his way back to where he'd started. After rechecking Bella's car, he went to the last place he could think of.

"Catherine! Hello!" he called as he made his way around the stones. "Bella!"

Bella, the girl he'd grown to rely on. The girl he needed in more ways than he'd realized until now. She wouldn't just leave, especially knowing that Catherine was hurt. Her car and bag were still at the cottage. She wasn't answering her phone, despite all the worried texts and calls. The thought that he was mirroring her ex-boyfriend came to mind, but he quickly shrugged it off. Danny just wished he knew she was safe, but everything inside him was saying she wasn't, and that thought shook him to his core. He needed her to be safe. She was the most important and amazing person. The last time he'd felt this way . . . who was he kidding? He'd never felt this way before. It was Bella. There was no other woman like her.

Danny envisioned her standing in front of him, her chocolate-brown eyes shining out at everything around them, the sun beating down on her golden curls. If the sun could speak, it would tell of finding its soulmate. Danny knew Bella was his match, his other side of the same coin, and now he wanted more than anything to tell her how he felt. Instead, he'd kept his feelings buried in the dark shade.

Standing next to Bella while watching Catherine and Bowen recite their vows, he saw a love he had never dreamed possible to be reserved for him. It had been there all this time, budding within him since they met, years before. After everyone had gone to bed the night before, he'd contemplated talking to Bella again, only this time less cheeky and more honest. Maybe there was a chance she felt the same way. She had put up with him for a long time, and she hadn't dated anyone since he'd moved into her flat. Though they both had flirtatious personalities, the chemistry between them wasn't something he could brush off. More than once he'd caught her looking at him, felt a spark when they accidentally touched. Nah. Sparks were flying everywhere, and he was the dumbest man alive to have waited so long to say anything.

But she was his sister's best friend, and at one time, they had been too much alike. He'd known he couldn't handle dating someone as fickle as him. However, both he and Bella had changed over the years. When he'd last returned to Ireland, seeing Bella had rekindled a raging fire in the cold emptiness he carried inside. Now he might never have the chance to tell her how he felt. She could be hurt somewhere, or worse.

Wide-eyed, he kept up his search, doing his best to push the terrifying thoughts into the far crevices of his mind, wanting more than anything to snuff them out completely. He stopped and gazed out over the empty fields surrounding the stones. Wiping his brow with the back of his hand, he tried to decide on his next move. He could no longer smell the strawberries she'd marked him with the night before. God, she smelled good. He would give anything to have that lingering scent back.

A soft melody sounded. It was faint at first but grew as the wind carried it right to his ear before ceasing all at once. He snapped his attention to the forest far in the distance. The very look of it drove an acute chill into his gut. The darkness and twisted trees created an eerie aura he'd rather not explore. Another thought came to him, and he slapped his hand through the air as though fanning it away. Bella wouldn't have gone in there in a million years. At least, not voluntarily.

Suddenly, small flashes of lightning broke through the blackness of the forest. Blinking, he took half a step forward before breaking into a run. It didn't look like Catherine's fire magic, but he had to be sure it wasn't something harming her or Bella. By the time he reached the edge of the forest, the flashes had stopped but music was playing again. A strange, soft sound. He didn't recognize the sound of the instrument.

Though alarmed by the alluring music, Danny couldn't resist the compelling urge to find its origin. It was so beautiful, and his body desperately wanted to meet it. He needed to meet it, but his mind screamed *danger*, reminding him this was the black forest. His sister had told him it belonged to faeries, and he would be opening himself up to their wrath if he trespassed even one step inside. He looked back at the distant stone ruins and the open fields. Bella and Catherine were nowhere to be seen. As far as he could tell, the black forest was the only clue he had to find them, and with his brother-in-law lying comatose at the cottage, it was up to him. In one swift movement, he turned and went inside.

It was just as Catherine had described: truly pitch black. He felt his jaw drop. He couldn't see one speck of the sky through the forest ceiling, and shadows layered the entrance behind him. The thick air was hard to breathe, and his pulse sped up the deeper he walked. Ahead, the music still played.

Then a startling, pounding noise erupted, shaking the ground. Danny grabbed one of the darker shadows next to him and was grateful it turned out to be a tree. The earth continued shivering. The vibration seemed to be resonating the strongest from a distance behind him, near the forest's entrance. Danny suddenly envisioned an irritable giant stuffing his socks and other articles of clothing into the opening to block out the insufferable light disturbing his sleep. Danny hoped there were no such things as giants. It was bad enough that he could become prey to all manner of different faeries at any moment.

The earth was still again. He pushed himself forward and continued walking for what felt like an hour until the music returned. It sounded nearer this time. He was getting closer. The thick air turned cold, and he wondered how that was possible in such a confined space. It nicked at him through his thin shirt and slacks. Though his feet were warm, they ached in his shoes from the long walk. His hands were extra sensitive to the cold as a result of the frostbite he'd suffered on a ski trip as a child. He wrapped them in his shirt and brought them to his mouth so he could blow hot air into his palms.

Light appeared in the distance, but as he drew near, he felt no warmth from it. There was a small, empty clearing, but the music was here, at its loudest. He shivered as he listened. The longer he stood and listened the colder he became. His eyes drooped, and he landed in the dirt with a smile on his face. He was one with the music.

6

Danny woke with a start. Hovering over him was a beautiful woman with a wild mess of long red hair. Her eyes were the darkest he'd ever seen, her face expressionless. Scrambling back and away from under her, he eyed her cautiously.

"Who are you?" he asked.

The woman didn't move or speak.

He glanced around for any more surprises, but the area was bare of any other soul, much to his relief. "Who are you?" he repeated, combing back some of the hair that had fallen into his face. He could barely move his cold fingers.

When she didn't respond, he clumsily stood up, keeping his gaze fixed on her.

"Look, if you're lost, we can help each other. It would help if you spoke. Are you lost?"

The woman slowly shook her head.

"Great, well, I'm actually lost, but you might have guessed that. Happen to see any other women in this forest since you've been here?"

The red mass surrounding the entirety of her body shifted only slightly when she calmly nodded.

"Oh my God, really? Where? Um, just point in the right direction." The words rushed out in a jumble. He didn't know if she was telling the truth, or if the women she claimed to have seen were the ones he was seeking, but this was a start.

The strange woman slowly lifted her arm, creepily long and slender, and pointed to her left with her index finger.

"Thank you, thank you!" He moved to leave but then stopped short. "Can you get home okay? I mean, you can come with me if you want."

Once again, she slowly shook her head and extended her arm straighter still.

"Thanks again," he said with a small grin, then disappeared down the path.

Catherine felt as if she'd been walking all day, but time wasn't the same here, so she tried not to think about how much of it she was losing. It was dark now, but much to her relief, not as black as the black forest. There was a heavy mist in this part of the forest though, and it stung her eyes as she walked into it. Eventually, the burning lessened enough for her to squint through her watery gaze, and what she saw startled her. The mist was behind her, and ahead was an elaborate glass structure. It seemed to span for miles, intertwined with the surrounding trees. The clearer her vision became, the more she could see that the glass was piled on top of itself, beautiful level upon beautiful level in an unearthly angular design that would make an architect weep. A faerie castle, surrounded by and entwined with its realm.

Catherine gaped. The castle was like nothing she had ever imagined in her wildest thoughts of the fae realm. She wondered who lived in such a place. A multitude of fae? Or was it set aside for fae nobility? She had to tear her eyes away from the glorious glass, glimmering in the light of the moon and stars. Much of the light bounced off the dozens of lakes in front of her. The place was calm and quiet and perfectly still, but she could feel paranoia creeping up on her, and had the alarming sense that a pair of eyes was locked on her every move. She swallowed once and gritted her teeth. She had to continue.

As Catherine walked, she noticed her feet never made a sound. She would have thought herself deaf if it weren't for the fierce sound of her blood pumping in her ears and the quick and heavy breaths she tried but failed to silence. A small gust of wind directed her onto a dark path, away from the one leading to the glass castle. She followed her instincts and went where it pushed.

To her right were a few ponds. Given how dirty her feet were, she longed to dip them in the clear waters but ignored the small desire. She needed to stay focused. Ahead was a wall of bushes that reached far above her head. A dead end. She spied a narrower path running perpendicular to the one she was on, directly in front of the bushes. A left turn would take her back toward the castle, but a nagging feeling was pulling her in the other direction. She took the hard right, and as soon as she did, the night scene shifted its space so that a large room opened up to her literally out of thin air. She gasped and stepped back, stunned for a moment before she kept going, until something moved in the corner. She stopped.

A tall figure disappeared through another entrance. She caught sight of a long black braid. "Wait," she called, but it was gone.

She didn't bother giving chase. Instead, she gazed around the space. Wall-hanging tapestries of threaded silver inlaid with various floral designs covered the entire room. One tapestry gave the illusion of covering an entire wall but was actually set in closer to the middle of the room. Catherine peeked behind it.

"Bowen," she gasped. On a body-sized table that resembled a medieval stretcher lay her beloved, just as pale and seemingly lifeless as before. "Bowen, can you hear me?" She caressed his chiseled chin. Nothing. Not the slightest response. She cursed under her breath, fighting back rage. She couldn't tell if he was dead, but her heart told her not to give up.

"If you die, I'll follow after you," she whispered. She pressed her lips to his cold earlobe. *Soon*, she thought. After saving Bella, she would lie down beside her husband and wait for death, but she wanted to do so back at the cottage. *How can I get you back there? How did you get here?*

"Druid woman," said a smooth voice behind her.

Catherine snapped around to meet it. "You!" It was the silvery fae she'd encountered in the woods. "Why did you take him?" she rasped.

The fae woman smiled, and her smile was every bit as unsettling as her chilling frown. "You're brave to come here."

"I want my husband returned to me," she demanded. "You have no right to do this."

"I am queen, and I can do as I wish within my lands."

The word queen caught Catherine off-guard, but she quickly recovered. "You took him from my lands, and I demand you give him back to me."

The queen walked toward her—the movement was closer to gliding—all the while not taking her eyes off her, as though she were a cruel cat surveying her prey. Catherine wondered if it was hunger or play she saw in the fae's frightening stare and hoped it was just her imagination on both counts. The eerie woman stopped suddenly, just a few steps away from her, but even that was uncomfortably close. "I do not part with my collections easily."

Collections? The word crawled over Catherine like a spider.

"I see the power you carry, and I want to taste it," she whispered. Even her voice was silvery.

Catherine flinched and narrowed her eyes.

"Follow," the queen commanded, and left the room through a side door that had appeared when she said the word.

Without thinking, Catherine followed her outside and was quickly surrounded by tall yet less-towering trees than the others she'd seen there. Even in the darkness, their leaves were vibrant with color. The ground crunched noisily under her feet now with thick layers of red, yellow, and green leaves. Some much shorter and drooping trees were scattered there as well, their long, vine-like leaves brushing the forest floor much like a weeping willow. They walked for a short distance before the fae stopped just above a black pond. Catherine almost missed it. In the darkness, it looked like a void she could fall through.

"Dip into the pool so I might have a taste." The faerie's voice was predatory now.

Catherine cringed and gazed into the liquid black hole. "I'm not going in there without assurance Bowen will be freed."

"Your lover is in this pond. If you find him, I will let him leave."

Catherine's mind spun. "What are you saying? How can he be in there but also behind us?"

The queen waved her hand over the pond, and it rippled in the small wind to reveal a ghostly figure sitting against something within the murky water. He was staring off into the nothingness that surrounded him. Catherine's breath caught in her throat. Bowen.

"My pond holds his spirit. Retrieve it, and he is yours once more." Her laughing violet eyes gave away the truth. Bowen was indeed in the pond, but where?

Catherine hesitated, looking back and forth from the pond to the faerie woman. "You'll return his body too?"

She nodded lightly.

"I have your promise?"

"It is done without my hand. If you retrieve his soul out of the pond, his body will return to where it was stolen from. I swear it."

Catherine didn't trust her, but still, she had to try. If there was even a small chance that this was real, and that was really Bowen's spirit in the pond, she couldn't just walk away. She folded her fingers into a fist. "All right."

She took a deep breath and stepped forward into the water. Its cold caresses reached higher and higher as she walked until the ground fell out from beneath her, and she sank. Completely submerged, and without the celestial light above to guide her, Catherine felt as though a blanket had been thrown over her head. A cold and heavy blanket. Feeling the scarf on her head slip, she managed to grab it before it floated off, and stuffed it into her skirt pocket. After a moment, her eyes adjusted. Below was a dull blue light, and down she dived to follow it. As she passed through a thick layer of bubbles, she found herself able to breathe within the water. She gasped with shock and relief but didn't slow down.

The blue light grew brighter, allowing Catherine to see what lay at the bottom of the pond. There was seaweed and glowing blue fish weaving in and out of sparkling treasure. Most of it looked silver, though she couldn't be sure since everything was tinted the same dark shade of blue. She swam over to examine some of the closest pieces, her inner archaeologist working. They spoke to her of times long past, and lands buried deep inside the earth or swallowed by the sea. Chests of jewels winked at her and glinted off neighboring piles of weaponry—swords, axes, jeweled and crude daggers, and more. Heaps of wealth.

As she passed over the last glimmering pile, the sparkling decreased dramatically, and her gaze fell on something else. Bones. There were loose and assembled ones, as well as many whole skeletons. Some looked human, some fae, but others didn't match anything Catherine recognized. The word "collections" resurfaced in her mind, and she began to fear for more than Bowen's spirit. She swam more quickly. Who knew how long she had before the water decided to add her to the pile of bones?

Something large moved in and then out of sight in the distance, and her stomach clenched in alarm. Another flutter in the water to her right, then to her left. *Is something living down here?* She suddenly imagined a monster gnawing on bones and discarding them into piles. Catherine's mind raced against her heart. At this rate, she didn't know which would win.

Suddenly, long tentacles swooped out from the dark water and grabbed her feet. Electric shocks attacked her fingertips. On instinct, Catherine directed her fire power at the creature. Beams of lava cut through the water like explosives. The creature fought back and lashed out two more tentacles that tried to wrap around her waist, but it only succeeded in locking more of her legs in its slithery coils. This action brought the creature out of hiding and into the blue light. It was massive, with two beady black eyes directly next to each other and a long snout. Its arched back glowed with blue bulbs of light, each pulsating and releasing a substance into the water. Catherine didn't have time to decipher where the creature's many limbs originated from. It thrashed around, knocking her every which way.

Catherine released another burst of magic and managed to burn off one of its limbs, which sent the creature into a rage. It whirled back and let out a rumbling groan. She freed one limb, then another. Before she could even register it, she was swiftly pinned down on top of piles of bones, one arm behind her back. She wiggled, pulled, and twisted, almost dislocating her shoulder, but no matter how hard she tried, she couldn't release it. She knew she couldn't muster up enough magic to win the fight with only one hand, only enough to keep the monster at bay, and not for long. The creature's light bounced off of something that caught Catherine's eye. It was just over the side of the bone pile, under a stack of three skeletons still mostly assembled.

Sending wave upon heavy wave her way as it wildly moved in the water, the creature roared angrily before rearing backward, preparing for the final strike. With her free hand, Catherine reached, stretching herself in a way she'd never thought possible. The creature raged a second more and shot toward her. At the same moment that one of the bones underneath her snapped, she grabbed the shining object just in time to meet her attacker with the end of a silver glaive. It froze, the blade rooted deep between its beady eyes. She showed no mercy, pushing her fire through the weapon. The flame bolt split the creature in two. The tentacles relaxed and released their hold, unpinning her instantly.

Catherine floated, stunned, breathing heavily. The idea of being out of breath but still breathing underwater wasn't processing well in her brain, but her body registered having just survived a deadly attack. She quickly gathered her senses and continued swimming. She didn't know how many strange creatures lived down here with the bones and treasure, and she wasn't about to wait for any more to find her.

There had been no sign of Bowen's spirit so far, only fish, large fish monsters, treasure, and bones. But no spirits. *Where could he be?* She tried to remember if there was anything but murky water in the image the fae queen had shown of Bowen, anything that could help her find the same place, but nothing came up. She swam around some more, her worry increasing.

She finally spotted him. Relief washed over her. He was sitting with his back against a chest of jewel-hilted daggers. "Bowen," she called as she approached. He didn't move. "Bowen, can you hear me? Listen, get up." She touched his ghost-like hand and flinched. It was cold and mossy, like the water. It was the first time she'd ever disliked his touch. That, and the whole situation unsettled her. She pursed her lips as she swallowed hard. Determined, she tried again, this time resting her hand on his arm. "Come with me, right now."

"Catherine?" His deep voice rippled through the water and then through her. It sounded distant and lost.

She summoned all of her strength of persuasion. "It's me, Bowen. Listen." Still he looked at her with only the slightest hint of recognition. "I need you to follow me. Here, take my hand." When he didn't move, she grabbed hold of both his hands, entangling their fingers.

"Come on!" Overwhelmed, she tugged in frustration. He didn't budge at first, but a few attempts got him moving. As she continued to coax him through the water, she had to keep checking to make sure he wasn't going to zone out completely again.

Though exhausted, Catherine swam as fast as she could, her fear of losing Bowen overtaking everything else. They passed through the bubbling wave, and she knew the surface was just ahead. She held her breath tightly in her chest. The ascent seemed to be taking a little too long. She pressed on. There were no lights to confirm the surface was there, but it couldn't be too much further. With Bowen in tow, she had to be moving more slowly. Puddles of doubt started to leak inside of her, and she was just on the edge of panic, about to turn back for air, when they splashed through the black surface. She emerged from the water to find that Bowen's hands were no longer in hers. Anxiety quickened and she looked back at the pond, gulping in a deep breath to dive back in.

"Your time is done."

Catherine whipped around to face the fae woman, who was waiting for her in the same spot she'd left her. "I had him! He was with me when I reached the surface. What have you done with him?"

The fae's alluring eyes widened in wonder, making Catherine feel as though she were a newly arrived relic at the museum.

"Those lines on your head," the fae said, her voice breathy. "That's why you still have your magic."

How could she know that? Catherine had forgotten she wasn't wearing her poorly-made scarf and hoped it was still in her skirt pocket. Soaking wet and shivering cold didn't cool the untamed heat flushing her cheeks. But she stared at the queen with clenched teeth, not knowing what to say. This fae was obviously involved in her recent trouble, but Bowen was her priority.

Violet eyes narrowed on her. "Return to my pond. It calls for you."

A flame rose inside Catherine's stomach, and her shivering ceased. "I'll never be part of your collection, and neither will Bowen. For the last time, where did he go?"

The fae turned to leave, but Catherine gave chase. A moment later she bounced off an invisible wall and fell back onto the leafy ground. She shot her hand in the queen's direction. Her firebolt blazed through the wall with ease and headed toward the queen, who spun around and fanned it aside, to hit one of the drooping trees.

To Catherine's disbelief, the bark shattered like glass. All of a sudden, it felt as if she were being torn from the inside out. She doubled over as the world around her shifted and dissolved. When she opened her eyes, the pain was gone, she was wearing her scarf, and she was dry. Before her was a standing mirror, elaborately decorated and melded within a tapestry-covered wall. It was shattered, but the pieces remained mostly stuck together, with only a few falling at her feet. Had the walk to the pond, and the pond itself, been a mere illusion?

There was movement, and Catherine snapped around just in time to block a silver gust of wind.

"You destroyed my collections!" the queen cried.

Catherine gasped. *Bowen! Where's Bowen?*

"I'm here." The deep voice echoed in her head and sounded close by. She looked behind her, but no one was there.

A painful strike to the back of her head brought a shooting white flash with it, and she fell to her knees, pressing the heels of her palms into her eyes as she cried out. Before she could recover, a swift kick to her ribs and another blow to her head sent her flat to the floor. She couldn't move, she couldn't think. The only thing she noticed was the oddly warm floor under her, and the vague sound of music following heavy footsteps, which stopped directly next to her.

"Be vigilant. She still has her power," she heard the queen say before everything went black.

7

PERCHED QUIETLY ON A TREE BRANCH, and out of sight from below, Bricius studied his new possession with discerning eyes. The human woman with golden curls and brown eyes stood, seemingly lifeless. Though she was chipped around the edges, to him, she was fascinating. Perfect, even. He could see something deep inside her soul, a light different than he'd seen in the other humans he'd watched wander into his realm over the centuries. He wanted to own not only her but that mysterious light as well. He wanted to make it his.

Something rustled, and the air shifted. Bricius nimbly jumped down the tree to land in a crouched bow. "Sire."

Loïc stood over him. Though his head was lowered, Bricius could feel the king's gaze scrutinizing him. "I've called for you more than once. Why have you kept me waiting?"

"Your queen bade me bring someone for her—"

"I'm aware, Bricius. That was before. What of now?" Loïc's voice was tight. Real golden feathers and tapered metal ones scraped against each other in his headdress.

"Forgive me. I have no excuse for my negligence."

He glanced up to see Loïc looking at the frozen beauty a short distance away. "I see," he mumbled. "Don't let it interfere with my orders again."

Bricius clenched his fingers tighter in his balled fists. "Yes, sire," he said, swallowing back the climbing frustration. He wanted to help Loïc succeed as quickly as possible so that he could spend all of his time here, watching her. Then something occurred to him. "Has Gwenaël done her part?"

A dark chuckle followed. "That she has. She still has the half-breed weakling wrapped around her finger. Though, she bores so easily, I don't know how much longer she'll continue. Regardless, everything is falling into place."

Many times, Bricius had witnessed how easily swayed Gwenaël could be. Her infamous boredom was the cause of many small fires that Loïc had put out with Judicaël over the centuries. Like Bricius, Gwenaël liked to collect things, to own them completely, as if she could somehow become them. They'd done this for as long as he could recall. Their interest in the outer realms never failed, even when some realms were closed off to them, or when they were suddenly forbidden to take anything or anyone out of them. Of course, among others who held the same curiosities and cravings, neither he nor the queen could abide by these rules. They simply had to know what was out there, and so their need grew with each guilty find.

Bricius lifted his head just as Loïc sighed and eyed him again. The king waved for him to rise. "Cadeyrn must not find you out of his realm. Make sure to keep yourself and your things hidden."

Bricius nodded. Cadeyrn was a noble king, much like Judicaël, but his emotions fluctuated less. Although Cadeyrn was willing to bend rules on occasion, he only ever did so for the good of all and never for desires considered small, such as his own. Loïc, on the other hand, understood his side of the fae like no other. He knew how strong the need for human energy was, and the need to own it entirely.

Bricius knew Loïc wasn't doing any of this for his subjects, though. He was using the divide to gain his own centuries-old desire: to be the high king. "I must wait." He lowered his voice to nearly a whisper. "I must wait for when there are fewer opposing fae, and until—" He looked away. "Until he is weaker. It will not happen until long after the war is won, but I can wait."

The first thing Bella noticed when she woke up was how little she could see. The darkness was as startling as the distant black forest had been the morning she'd been walking through the druid ruins. That was the last thing she could remember. How long had it been since then? The next thing she noticed was that she couldn't move. Her eyes wouldn't even dart from side to side, and her tongue wouldn't click inside her mouth. She was frozen, like one of the many living statues she'd passed in Dublin over the years. The difference was, she wasn't performing.

Fear squeezed her heart, and she wanted to scream, but her voice was also locked away. She tried to calm herself, reason with herself, anything to anchor onto a semblance of control. As her eyes adjusted, she could see gloomy trees and an overgrown forest floor ahead and in her peripheral vision. She tried to focus on anything that might connect her to her body.

A small wind swept over her, tickling her arms and raising the small hairs on her neck. Inwardly, she gasped from the sensation, then gave a grateful sigh. She wasn't as completely detached from her body as she'd feared. The nightmare was very real, but something similar to hope still remained.

Suddenly, a shadow dropped from the treetops not far from where she stood. From her current angle, she could see two tall figures from the corner of her eye. One was crouched, long limbs folded and steady in a bow. The other stood tall, hovering over the bent figure. Their voices were clear, but the words they spoke were unlike any language she'd ever heard before. Patiently, she listened to the rise and fall of their private conversation. The one standing had a voice like music, though something sinister lingered within it. The other's voice was slick, charming. Both seemed guarded in different ways.

Once more she tried to move her body, but nothing budged. This was magic. The place reeked of it. Cathy had warned her of the black forest, had told her all about her visit there last year. Maybe she was inside the faerie lands, and maybe that meant she wasn't too far away from her friend, and rescue. She hoped Cathy had found Mary without her. Maybe Bowen and Cathy were well again. Dan, too.

The thought of Dan sent a series of pangs through her chest, and if they could move, her lips would have been trembling. That moment with Dan in the dusty library kept replaying in her head. Maybe she could have broken the news better. Maybe she should have told him before they'd arrived, or maybe she should have just told him how much he meant to her. How much he'd always meant to her. "I'd rather you get to the point and say what you mean," she'd said to him. She'd waited for so long because the timing never seemed right. Now it was too late, and she felt like such a hypocrite.

The two figures separated, drawing her attention back. Then the servile one moved so quickly toward her that it made her insides squirm. The strong instinct to run beat at every muscle in her body, but nothing could break her free.

As the figure appeared out of the darker shadows, she shivered inwardly in terror as realization struck. It was the strange man she'd seen in the trees across from her car. Now that he was near, close enough that his breath was practically suffocating her, she perceived that the word strange didn't quite do justice to his startling, unearthly form.

He was definitely one of the fae. His sinister eyes, deceivingly charming smile, and broad shoulders were the only features that resembled those of a human man. When he leaned in, she thought for a moment that he was going to kiss her, but instead, he turned his head sideways to examine other parts of her. He was whispering to himself in slow, deliberate phrases she couldn't comprehend.

Trapped, she examined him in turn to distract herself from the unsettling sound of his words. His dark hair reminded her of a well-groomed black horse, and it was gathered into a long, sleek braid that hung casually over his shoulder. Jewels lined his ears almost all the way around, except for the pointed and slightly slanted tips. The shape of his profile was stunning, and his milk-white skin seemed to reflect whatever light was near.

Her body became tired. Her neck felt heavy, as though something was pulling on her hair, weighing it down. To Bella's horror, the fae turned back to her. His lips almost touching hers, he caressed her face as he stared deeply into her eyes. She didn't like the look he gave her as he did so. Panicked thoughts plagued her. Fear was taking hold. What did he want with her? Why was she there?

She shouldn't be here. She should be in Dublin, helping the children she took care of with their homework. Dublin, where Dan would be waiting for her at home. Waiting for her to tell him about her day, and then after a hearty meal, on most days they would talk until they both fell asleep. She'd become accustomed to the sound of his breathing when he slept, she could always hear him from his sofa bed if she didn't shut her bedroom door. She had to combat his different moods throughout the week because he was so bored, but he always wanted to spend time with her. That piece of knowledge made her eager to get home every day, no matter how much she enjoyed her job.

When the fae creature pulled away, Bella felt her mind slipping, as though passing through a thick fog. She fell deeper and deeper into her dark cage.

Danny's heart raced. He'd been walking awhile now, and he stumbled as a loud clanging followed by a terrible crash rang through the forest. He scurried to the large clearing ahead, and the sight made his jaw drop. People—*or fae,* he thought—and wild beasts were throwing blows at one another with steel weaponry and magic. Some needed neither and attacked with claw and bone.

His heart raced even faster at the sight of a smoky black steed snorting wildly. Sitting on its saddle was a figure hidden by a black cloak that hung so long it covered most of the horse's backside. The horseman held his right hand high in the air, and something dangled from it, but Danny couldn't see what it was from where he hid in the distance. It glowed in the gloomy evening, creating a path of light. The horse galloped around, encircling the battle. When it drew close enough that Danny could see the figure more clearly, his heart stopped. There was no head on the horseman's neck. Instead, it hung from his grasp, lighting the way. The ghostly light faded as the black steed turned full circle and galloped away, each step a burst of earth-rocking thunder.

Every fae the horseman passed fell to the ground, dead. Still crouched, Danny moved behind a large tree trunk for added precaution. Ruptures of light flashed with every clang and clatter, and finally, he grew used to seeing stars. The battle was coming to an end, and he needed to get away before anything scattered into the woods where he was hiding. Carefully, he slid backward and then continued in the direction in which the woman had pointed him. He walked and walked some more, his frazzled nerves keeping him alert.

The last thing he'd eaten was the wedding dinner, and his stomach had been aggressively protesting since that morning. Given his current level of discomfort, Danny knew he had to find something to snack on soon. Wondering the time, he took his phone out of his back pocket, thankful he hadn't lost it in the chaos. *Damn.* The battery was dead, and he wasn't wearing a watch. After stuffing the phone back into his jeans, he stopped, placed his hands on the back of his head, fingers clasped, and pulled. The stretch felt good in his back and chest, but the overall movement made his head feel loose on his shoulders. Combing his fingers through his messy hair in a few quick swipes, he continued walking.

How long had he been in the fae realm? He couldn't think straight. How long had he been walking? The forest seemed endless. It seemed that time passed differently here, but he didn't know for sure. Maybe his starving mind was just imagining things. Another stomach contraction forced him to stop against a tree. The pain was so precise, he could almost feel the ulcer forming as the acid burned. He'd ignored it too long. His stomach wouldn't be silenced anymore and wanted him to suffer for his neglect. With his head swimming, all he could do was wrap his arms around his middle and hope he spotted something, anything, to eat. Just for some relief, he'd even take something poisonous. At this rate, it wouldn't make a difference.

Sharp twigs took advantage of his plight and reached out like claws, scraping the backs of his hands as he struggled to remain standing. He winced and pulled away, then carefully dabbed his hand with his shirt. The bloodstain left behind was barely visible in the dark blue of the fabric, but in the glowing light of the faerie realm, what human eyes could discern much of anything?

He walked forward one step after another. If he could just keep walking, maybe somehow he would find them, one of them, Bella or Catherine. He needed to know that at least one of them was alive. Just then, as if the thought had conjured it, a woman's silhouette formed a short distance away, standing on the footpath. Only it wasn't a path any longer, but a hidden recess of the forest. Painfully aware of his condition, Danny wondered if he was delusional.

He stumbled over his feet and held onto another tree for balance. "Bella?"

If only it were actually her. More than anything he wanted to see her again. Through blurry vision, Danny could see her familiar frame just ahead, and as his vision cleared, he saw she was still as a statue with a vacant look in her eyes. He ran forward and grabbed both of her arms before he could fall again. "God, you're safe! I didn't think I'd ever find you!"

Feeling faint, he slumped over and took a few deep breaths, until the blood returned to his head. He planted his feet more securely into the ground and pulled his head up to look back at Bella, leveling his eyes with hers. Taken aback by the miles of distance in them, fear rose through his body. "Can you hear me?" he whispered.

She didn't flinch.

Danny tore his gaze away and searched frantically for any sign of injury or oddity. Gently tugging on her hair, he noticed the curly bulk felt impossibly heavy. He looked behind her and gaped at the sight. Golden tresses fell down her back and rolled on past the trees behind them, weaving and looping like the coils of a snake.

Bella was like an ice sculpture, frozen in stillness, skin cold, but she wasn't solid like ice. No, she was empty like a shell. A beautiful shell. Meeting her gaze again, he saw no light or any sign of life. Her unblinking eyes looked right through him and chilled him to the bone. A sudden eerie sensation filled the air right as Danny heard rustling behind him, and he quickly turned to meet it.

"Ah, it's you." An intruder entered the recess with slow, deliberate steps.

"Who the hell are you?" Danny narrowed his gaze. Light came from the approaching figure, and Danny saw a tall, lean male fae dressed in black. His ghostly-white face was framed with ebony-colored hair that hung down to his knees in one long braid.

"I'm this human woman's owner now."

Danny scowled. "She's no one's property." The fae wavered, then continued moving toward him. "You bastard," Danny muttered under his breath. His revulsion didn't seem to concern the fae.

"Call me Bricius." With disgust, he added, "I hate the way humans speak. All human languages. They're all the same. My name doesn't sound half as nice in your tongue." He shrugged. "And I can own whomever I want. Everyone can be manipulated." The fae casually folded one arm across his chest and cupped a pale cheek in the other as he eyed Danny with a blue stare.

Danny glanced at the vacant Bella before looking back at the being whose soul seemed to be the very hand of evil. "That's not true. You have her under some kind of control." His fists shook as he struggled to restrain himself.

Bricius tilted his head from side to side, seeming to ponder something. Danny gritted his teeth. "I might have, but nonetheless, she is mine, human. You don't belong here. Leave now, and I'll ignore you." He sighed exasperatedly. "Besides, I'm tired of degrading myself to speak on a level you'll understand."

"What do you want from her?" The fae's arrogance was

digging nails into the back of Danny's head, but he had to stay focused on Bella.

Bricius sighed heavily again. "I want her. She's my beauty to look at, whenever I want, and no one else's. I want everything from her." A force pushed Danny aside as the fae approached Bella's doll-like form and caressed the top of her head.

The sudden force pushed Danny off balance, and his phone slipped out of his pocket. He stumbled, and then—*crack.* The screen was toast beneath his shoe, but he didn't flinch. He only rolled his eyes back up, the daggers in them sharpened. "You can never have everything from her," he hissed.

"Yes, I can. I already do. She's here, isn't she?" His voice sounded tighter.

"Never. Because you're missing so much of her beauty, which I've already seen."

Bricius twisted his face in disdain as he looked at him. "Explain yourself, human."

Danny knew the fae could never understand, but still, his feelings overwhelmed him and came gushing out. "The way she walks, the sound of her voice when she speaks. Even the soft humming of whatever song she can't help but hum when she's cooking is beautiful to me." He couldn't restrain a small grin from escaping. "The way she ties her hair up with a pencil while she's reading. I could look at her for hours."

Bricius dropped his hand from Bella's head, and his brow wrinkled. "Tell me more."

Danny was just happy the fae had stopped touching her. *That's one step in the right direction.* "Bella has a way with people. Her laugh is contagious, and she's the sweetest woman you'll ever find." Danny inched closer to her as he spoke, hoping to keep the fae distracted. It was working. Bricius looked confused.

"But her most beautiful feature is her eyes, those two brown marbles that her bright spirit shines out from. But you've taken that away and left her trapped somewhere inside herself." He planted his feet directly in front of Bella's.

The smallest of grunts escaped the fae. "Fine then, I'll let her move around and speak if that will reveal more beauty, as you say." With a flick of his hand Bella's limbs twitched, and she blinked twice before the light behind her eyes returned and shined on Danny.

"Dan," she said, her voice groggy. She winced and grabbed her throat.

"Are you okay?" he asked, biting his lower lip. Bella shook her head and reached for his hand. "What's wrong?"

Bella didn't answer. Instead, she dipped her head onto his shoulder.

"Saying your name literally makes her sick." Bricius smiled. "You see, she can't do anything that displeases me, and her saying your name is one of those things." Danny glowered, but the fae paid him no mind. "Now, my beautiful human, walk around as you do and let me see how your beauty increases. Only, don't think you can leave. You're mine, remember."

Danny ignored him, focusing on getting Bella's attention. Her shoulders were shivering. "There, there, calm down," he whispered through her curls.

"My patience is waning, little human."

"She's hurting," Danny snapped. "Can't you see that?"

Bricius shifted his gaze out to the trees and tilted his head as if listening for something. Then he turned and nimbly hopped off on long legs through the night forest.

Danny felt relief spread through him but didn't waste any time. "Bella, hold yourself up. I have to pick up your hair so we can leave." He looked down at the coils of locks and heaved a worried sigh. "If I can."

"It's no use," she said. Her voice was back but tight with worry.

"Maybe if I carry some and you drag the rest? Would that hurt you, though?"

"No. Yes. I don't know, but I can't run away with you."

"What are you talking about?" Danny asked, grabbing both of her shoulders in protest. "He's gone. We have to at least try and get away."

"No," she said simply.

What the hell was wrong with her? Danny was stunned into silence for a moment. "But we've got to!" There was no other way. He wasn't giving up and leaving her.

"One step out of my cage and she'll fall asleep forever." The voice resonated through the air around them.

Bricius wasn't far.

"You see?" she gasped despairingly. "You can't rescue me. Just go and save yourself."

"I can't just leave you."

Bella pulled at her face and wrung her hands. Her dismay was palpable. "Unless you have some knowledge of fae magic or anything that can help, then this is the only option."

Suddenly, some words he'd read in one of Mary's books thundered back to him: *Escape is with earth magic or the magic of true love.*

Without thinking, Danny grabbed Bella by the waist.

"What are you doing?"

Ignoring her, he pressed their lips together. He paused just long enough to look into her eyes. She didn't resist. Her lips parted. She tasted like everything he'd ever wanted for his future.

Reunited, one kiss can turn the tide.

For a perfect moment, everything in the world melted away, and it was only them. Bella moved with him, and he with her. Hope and desire swirled together inside of him, and he wondered why they hadn't been doing this the whole time. So much time had been wasted not kissing.

She was the first to pull away, but only slightly. "Finally."

He opened his eyes. "Hmm?"

"I've been waiting for you to kiss me for eons."

He grinned. "I didn't know you wanted me to."

Bella grinned back. "It was a perfect goodbye kiss."

Danny's grin dropped to a frown. *Goodbye?* "Bella, I'm not ever saying goodbye to you. No. You don't believe we broke the spell?"

She snorted. "With a kiss?"

"Yes." He pulled her with him as he turned to leave.

"No!" she cried, tugging on his arm. "You can't! He said I'll fall asleep and then you won't be able to carry me with all of my hair."

He stopped and turned back to her. "Then I'll have to keep you awake."

Bella frowned doubtfully.

"More kissing might delay it longer." Quick as lightning, Danny leaped forward, grabbed the back of Bella's head with one hand, and kissed her again. This time, as if on cue, an invisible ripple ran out of Bella and through him. Unlocking his lips from hers and opening his eyes, he saw hers widen in surprise. "Run!"

Bella grabbed at her locks. "But my hair!"

"Just drag it," he said, bending to pick up as much as he could hold and run with at the same time. "We have to go before he gets back."

They stumbled away from the invisible cage and began to run. It was easier than Danny had expected. He looked behind them and couldn't believe what he was seeing. The long curls were somehow moving on their own, weaving and bouncing out of the way of the trees and any other obstacles in their path. He didn't have time to marvel, but Danny picked up speed with renewed confidence.

After bursting through a thicket bordering a small field, he ran across to get to the woods on the other side. He breathed heavily in the murky air that hindered his vision as he kept a tight grip on Bella and her locks. "Hurry," he rasped, fighting exhaustion as his muscles screamed. Each step he took added more wood to the fire that burned his lungs.

"I can't," she sobbed, trying to keep up. "Just leave me!"

Danny stopped and spun around to take hold of both of her arms. "Do you ever want to see another human again?" Bella's eyes were downcast as she shook her head, and she sobbed even more loudly. "Your parents? Catherine? Do you hear me, Bella?" His hands trembled as he shook her.

"Yes!" she burst, meeting his gaze. "Of course I do, Dan! Stop!" He let her shove him enough to grip his shirt tightly. "Just stop it!"

He bit his lip, trying to calm his voice. "Then you need to keep going, and move as fast as you can."

Something inside of him hurt deeply at the sight of Bella's eyes lacking their usual shimmery and cheery radiance, now absorbed by misery and despair. "Dan."

"Just focus on staying awake, and I'll keep us moving," he said. Gently squeezing her arms kept his hands from continuing to tremble. "You can do this. I'm with you." He kissed her again, and the ripple passed through them once more. He would kiss her all night and day if that's all it took to stop the sleeping death from taking her, but he couldn't assume their love alone would save her. No, they had to get out of here.

Bella released her grip on his shirt before she fell into his arms and onto his chest. Her tears smeared his grungy shirt. "Run, then," she mumbled.

Danny soundly kissed the blonde mess of curls on top of her head before pushing himself away, grasping her hand, and breaking into a sprint, dragging her behind him. He would save her, even if it meant almost killing them both.

8

CATHERINE'S HEART swelled in her chest as she looked from Bella and Danny standing on her left, to Bowen on her right. A familiar cough directly ahead caught her attention. The other three were facing behind her to see the orange setting sun casting a golden glow everywhere.

"Everything is woven together," Mary said with a knowing smile. "The heavens shine on you, and they never lie."

Still at her side and facing the sunset behind her, Bowen held her around the waist in a tight grip. As she leaned forward she rested her cheek on his bicep, and she held on, reveling in his touch. "I just want things to be left as they are," Catherine whispered.

"Only some things stay the same forever."

Catherine looked up, bumping his chin slightly with the top of her head, and their eyes met. "How do you know that?"

He smiled down at her. "I just do," he replied quietly, keeping the conversation just between them.

Catherine shook her head. She couldn't understand the

meaning behind his or Mary's cryptic words. "Why didn't we get forever?"

The world shifted, and she and Bowen were back in their wedding bed, wrapped around each other and the white sheets.

"We will."

"I hate that you're so optimistic when everything is so blatantly bleak," she said with a scowl, and stabbed her chin into her folded arms.

Bowen rubbed the length of her back with his fingers, and it sent pleasant chills throughout her body. He let out a soft sigh behind her. "That it may be, but it won't always."

"What if we die? Won't it be then?" Heartache seemed never-ending.

"No, because we'll be together. It's still forever. Nothing can take away our forever," he said gently, but Catherine just frowned. "Do you believe me?" he asked, leaning over her shoulder and meeting her eyes.

"Will you believe me if I say yes and no?" Bowen's warm chest heaved with a small laugh. "It's just not the same, Bowen. I wanted life with you."

He settled into her back and rubbed his chin into the curve of her neck. "I know." After a moment he added, "Maybe if we fight hard enough, we'll get it."

"I'm fighting, but it's not enough. And I'm alone."

"It's enough, and if it isn't, it'll become enough. Your energy is different from everyone's. You're like an apple that looks like an apple but smells like a peach."

She rolled over on her back and met his laughing gaze. "I truly hope so."

"And you're not alone."

"Where are you, then?"

"Here." Catherine opened her mouth to protest, but he beat her to it. "Always here." He tapped above her left breast. "And here." He nudged her forehead with his. "You have the gift of the oak to turn your will into power. Stop trying to normalize your new surroundings, and embrace them instead." He rested his forehead against hers, his soft curls pushed just above.

How could she possibly embrace death? Especially his death? The world was slipping again, and they were back in the setting sun. Bowen's consuming warmth was never ceasing. It calmed her quivering heart as she watched the last of the orange sunlight mix with the dark blue of the sky and dim to soft shades of pink and purple. "I love you," she whispered, tightly shutting her eyelids. "And I want apples and peaches now."

He laughed, and oh how she basked in his laugh.

Catherine's eyes snapped open, tearing her from her dream and throwing her headlong into the waking world where she was surrounded by dozens, if not hundreds, of fae. She found herself standing in the middle of a giant room, her arms shackled together in front of her. The shackles pushed jaggedly every which way against her skin. She could already see bruises forming. Her clothes looked torn further, but the makeshift scarf remained tightly wrapped around her scarred, bald head. A dull ache penetrated deep inside of it and resonated with the burning ache on the surface, but not even the pain could distract her from the extreme exposure she felt from being the center of attention. All present were either looking at her with stern gazes or talking among themselves while glancing at her. An alarmingly loud hum filled the room.

With the exception of a few smaller creatures, these faerie people seemed to be the same kind of fae as the woman Catherine had met earlier. *Was it still the same day?* Some of these smaller ones had wings and hovered over the room, while others stood quietly with folded arms and gruff expressions. She didn't see any resembling the small creature she'd met on her first venture into the faerie realm. Mainly, this crowd was full of noble-looking courtiers, elegant and tall. Most of the men had clean-shaven faces, except for a few with blond beards that stuck close to their skin. Scanning the room, she spotted some with thicker, longer beards cropped around their necks in a circular style, giving them a more mature appearance and masculine demeanor.

Their clothing was undeniably woven from the richest of fabrics. They shimmered and caught her attention with every movement. The beautiful yet eerie material was like a moving element, with twinkling prisms, gritty earth, or silvery stone. Each one reflected the light. The women looked and moved like goddesses, their sultry bodies covered in robes that draped over them like tapestries waiting to unveil works of art. Catherine felt heat rise in her face as she looked down at her torn clothes again, and this time noticed her dirty bare feet, which were leaving sweaty footprints on the cold floor.

Behind the fae was a large arching entrance that rose at least three stories high in the glass wall. The room wasn't just big. Every wall, even the floor, was nothing but ornate, inlaid with various intricate and floral designs exquisitely stenciled into the glass surfaces. Catherine noticed some of them depicted the four seasons and specifically liked autumn and winter for their high winds, but she was drawn more to summer for its elaborate style of the sun. High above was a cathedral ceiling, and as she examined it further, she gasped. It suddenly phased out, revealing the morning sky above, streaked with reds and yellows. The walls did the same, and she twirled around, trying to catch every angle until they changed to some sort of in-between mode where only the stencil designs were visible.

Stopping mid-twirl with the crowd mostly to her back, Catherine saw an empty glass throne at the other end of the room facing her. The shining chair seemed to judge her, its foreboding vibes wafting her way. The walls and ceiling shifted again, returning to the glass. Changing between modes caught light from the horizon and after it closed from the outside, the bouncing light glimmered everywhere before disappearing completely. It reminded her of the glass castle she'd seen before.

Suddenly realizing that one fae was scrutinizing her more than the others, she adjusted her stance uncomfortably. This fae stood tall with the majesty of a great elk but the gaze of a bird of prey. Trying to distract herself, she continued to take in her surroundings. More than once the wall-shifts made her jump. Her nerves were rattled.

Moments later, a tall fae with broad shoulders and a trim waist moved through the room. With the crowds behind her blocking her view, she hadn't caught a glimpse of where he'd come from. All eyes were on him, including hers. She noticed that, though his face was hairless, he had more masculine features than the rest of the fae. As he strode toward her, the humming of the room instantly ceased. Catherine watched his elegant form stop and turn. He scanned the fae with an authoritative air before turning once more and continuing on his way. Each step he took, each shift in the unearthly fabric he wore that moved like ocean waves breaking against rocks and sand in slow motion, only emphasized his natural—or rather, unnatural—beauty. Glowing white hair trailed far behind him like a translucent cloak. Every fiber of Catherine's being was desperate to escape his lording presence. Everything about him was eerie. She briefly glanced at her chains again. Where was the weakest link?

The faerie lord moved past her and gracefully seated himself on the throne. His steel-gray eyes, glazed in frost, reflected her image, momentarily trapping Catherine's breath. Then, as if bored, this apparent king sighed, and his gaze shifted to the other fae still shooting daggers her way.

"Why have I been called to your castle, Loïc? Why have you brought me this druid woman?"

"My king." Loïc stepped forward and bowed. His alarming eyes were as black as the inside of the black forest but were framed with a ring of pale yellow. His head was completely covered by a golden headdress of long, intricate feathers. Some looked hardened like actual gold. They sprinkled the tops of his shoulders and fanned up and spiked out directly behind him. "It is from her that the lock came, and I've delivered her to you for judgment."

Catherine's eyebrows spread up high on her forehead. What could she possibly be judged for? This was ridiculous, she'd done nothing but defend herself. "There are others in this realm of fae who deserve judgment for theft and kidnapping." She glowered at Loïc, who sneered.

The king widened his eyes and straightened. "Druid woman." Catherine looked back at the beautiful king. "Since you understand our speech, and throw such accusations in my court, tell me, what misdeeds have you suffered?"

She'd forgotten she could understand other languages as her own due to her magic, as she'd first discovered the year before. Addressed directly by the king, Catherine felt small again, but she raised her voice in confidence, hoping justice would serve and she'd be rewarded for truth. "I came here to find my friend, who was taken without a trace. Then I discovered my oathing stone stolen. The signs pointed to your realm. I was then attacked twice, and discovered that my husband, who lay dying in our home, was also stolen after I left." She swallowed to steady her voice and continued. "A fae queen tried to trap him in her mirror, and lured me in after him for the same purpose."

Loïc scowled.

The king turned to him. "Is this true? Is Gwenaël to blame for these crimes?"

"My king, Judicaël, this human lies, of course." Loïc laughed mockingly, gesturing at her. Despite his unearthly features, Catherine thought he seemed the most human in the crowd of fae.

"Does she? Or is Gwenaël too ashamed to face me? How can this druid woman know of our only queen?"

"My queen was the one who caught her wandering dangerously in our forests, setting fires and disturbing our realm, my king. Gwenaël recognized her magic, and so did I, as belonging to the lock."

Lock? Catherine felt a ball knotting up in the bottom of her stomach. That was the second time he'd mentioned that word. Furrowing her brow, she desperately wished her ability was invisibility, at least long enough to escape.

Judicaël leaned back in his throne. "Hmm." His head remained still, but his gaze drifted to her. Catherine could feel her face pale. "In all my existence I have never come across any human not raised here who could understand our speech." He stood, gracefully descended the two steps, and walked straight up to her, his eyes never leaving her face. "Your magic is powerful, and," he came closer, so close that his translucent garments almost touched her feet, "elegant." He tilted his head and stared curiously into her eyes. His steely gaze sent chills from her neck down her spine.

Catherine couldn't understand where this beautiful and frightening king saw elegance in her. Afraid to speak to the fae creature so close in proximity, she shifted and averted her eyes, and gave a small nod.

"Are you afraid?" he whispered. His cold breath chilled her cheeks.

She met his eyes but couldn't answer.

"You should be."

Catherine's pulse raced at his words, not because of their meaning but because of the eerie, melodic notes that hung off each syllable. Music in the fae realm was just as unearthly as the fae themselves, and apparently so was their language, their very voice. It was its own kind of spell. What kind of magic spell was this king's voice carrying?

"Your majesty, please," she implored, finding her own voice. "Let me go find my family, and we'll never return here."

He closed his eyes, and she could breathe for a moment. But only a moment. The icy gaze returned to hold her. "You have already been here once and now return. How can I trust your words? It is because of your lock of hair, which holds only a fraction of your power, that all of my lower kingdoms are in turmoil."

What? Catherine couldn't believe what she was hearing. That's what they were calling "the lock?" Her hair was causing turmoil?

King Judicaël slowly backed away. "I'm not inclined to give you what you want. You are a criminal—"

"I've done nothing wrong!" She immediately regretted her outburst.

"Ah," he said, his voice even more invariable than before. "A civil war is on your head, and it is by that crime that you'll be judged."

"Please! I've told you the truth," she begged. "How is a lock of my hair causing a war?"

"Silence!" His garments billowed around him as he waved his hand. "Loïc has already spoken for you."

Catherine couldn't push the rising panic down any longer. She leaned forward and heaved, but having had nothing in her stomach for an unknown span of time, only burning bile forced its way out of her mouth. So much for elegance. She couldn't think straight, feeling everything and nothing at the same time. Her body pushed and poked her as it slowly receded and closed in on her broken spirit.

"I've decided to stay until the battle ends in the north, Loïc."

Loïc nodded. "Yes, my king." Then he gestured with his chin, signaling someone she couldn't see to gather up "the woman," now a pitiful version of the pillar of strength she'd once embodied.

"She stays with me." Judicaël brought all movement to a halt with one look. He motioned with his hand, and another fae rushed up, apparently one of the king's personal attendants. The fae removed Catherine's binds only to shackle her arms, this time behind her back in thicker chains. These were much heavier than she could bear, and she painfully crumbled to one knee. She began feeding off of her growing anger and glared at Loïc.

The fae's gaze darted away from her, and when the smug grin fell from his snake-like face, she cheered internally. He was obviously deceitful. How could the high king not see it? Or was she just that perceptive?

Loïc's voice shook. "Judicaël, she is too dangerous. You can't allow her to remain here. She can't help but be drunk on the power she wields."

Catherine couldn't stop herself from shouting, "No, you're wrong!" With the return of the humming from the crowd, her voice didn't carry far, and no one seemed to notice she'd spoken. She'd never asked for this. She didn't crave power. All she wanted to do was save her loved ones and go home. These strange beings of the faerie realm didn't know her at all, and yet they judged her. This wasn't right. They weren't right. No one was listening to her. How could she defend herself if no one listened? The frustration and anger boiled inside, and she wanted to scream, cry, and fight all at once.

Loïc waited a moment, but when Judicaël didn't acknowledge him, he continued desperately, "I thought it was for me to officially handle any humans in our realm as per your law?"

The high king whipped around, swiftly pushing his garments behind him in one motion. "Loïc!" His eyes were stern, daring Loïc to question him more.

Loïc continued. "Cadeyrn is the one who has taken it upon himself to defy you and your laws. He is against you and clearly desires to overthrow you. The owner of the lock, this pathetic woman," he gestured to Catherine with a sneer, "could be his spy. It may be best if she isn't able to gather any information she could gain in your presence outside of this trial."

Catherine guffawed humorlessly. "This is no trial. This is a spectacular performance of hearsay."

Still no one listened to her. Judicaël's stare relaxed for a moment before it sharpened even more. In his luminous form he summoned a dark song, which spiraled up through his throat and out past his lips. The sound made Catherine want to tunnel out of the room by any means, but the shackles served their purpose well. She only hoped his will was completely his own and not a tool for the vindictive Loïc he was punishing.

The song became visible to the naked eye as it engulfed Loïc in a gray mist. He instantly fell to his knees and begged for forgiveness, bowing his head and placing a hand across his blackened heart. Judicaël eased the volume, and the song fluttered backward, like birds quieting for sleep, until it disappeared completely.

"Rise, and find your queen to tell her both of you have distressed me this day."

Loïc glanced hatefully at Catherine before he rose and stalked past the hushed crowd and out of the court through the large arch.

Without looking her way, Judicaël waved to his guard who was still behind Catherine. She gasped as the guard heaved her back to her feet to be pushed out of a side entrance and down a glass staircase.

Besides the incredible physical strain that it was for her to walk with the heavy shackles binding her wrists at her back, it took all of her remaining mental stability to convince herself she wasn't going to fall to her death every time she took a step. The illusion the glass castle created was powerful, and she was thankful every time the glass became actual walls and floors. The guard then directed her down a connecting hallway, which intersected with a short ascending staircase. At the top were windows on either side of a narrow landing, and through them, Catherine could see a vast landscape of hills, forests, and grasslands. Everything was shrouded in varying levels of colorful fog, especially the forests, which the fae realm owned in abundance. Startling her from the view, the guard pushed her forward through a door that she'd thought was a mirror.

It opened up into a large, mostly empty room. It was hardly the dark and foreboding cell she'd imagined her prison would be.

Stunning furniture made of multiple tree limbs emerged from beneath the glass floor. The bed looked like a giant nest of colorful leaves, four-cornered glass pillars snaked around the branches holding it up. There was also a glass chair fused with a wide tree trunk, which continued up through the arching tower and out of the ceiling.

Sweating and exhausted, Catherine gazed at the room in awe. The guard gave her one last shove and left. Without his aid, she fell to the floor under the weight of the increasingly heavy shackles, far from the bed and chair. The glass shifted, and she cringed at the sight of the horrifyingly steep drop beneath her. With some precise maneuvering, she adjusted her head so she was looking at the ceiling instead of the floor, but that didn't stop her from jerking when the glass shifted again and it seemed as though the room had disappeared and she was floating in the sky. Eventually, she resorted to shutting her eyes and trying to conserve her energy. What was left of it.

Being in this realm was surely a test of her endurance, and a way to see how much power she really stowed inside herself. She would have never imagined her power would keep her alive while being so heavily drained. The question was, how much power remained? How much longer was she going to live?

Bowen. Was he alive, or had his spirit been just another illusion to trap her? Catherine let out a shaky sigh, and tears fell freely down the sides of her face and into the loose fabric strips of the scarf. She missed her husband deeply and wished more than anything that if she died, she would slip into a dream of him and never wake up.

9

CATHERINE DIDN'T DREAM of Bowen, and she did wake up. The sky was dark now, and the moon was only just gaining its bewitching light. With less difficulty than before, she rolled over, but her stomach groaned and ached more in this position, so she rolled back. For the first time since arriving in the fae realm, she felt the hunger eating away her stomach lining.

As if the fae had heard her thoughts, the door to her strange dungeon opened and a beautiful fae woman with long blonde hair and alarmingly blue eyes walked in. She didn't smile, but she didn't frown. Her face was entirely devoid of emotion. Catherine watched her carry a tray with two bowls full of berries varying in size and color but equally mouthwatering to look at. Bread and a tall glass of water filled the rest of the tray space. As soon as the beautiful creature set it down next to her on the floor, she spun on her toes and left just as quickly as she'd arrived. Because her arms were bound behind her, Catherine bent her head down to eat as many berries as she could without choking, throwing manners to the wind. She didn't have the time, luxury, or the physical ability to use them. She needed her strength, and she needed it fast if there was any hope of escaping.

Her cheeks warmed as she remembered what had happened at the royal court. She couldn't wrap her head around that so-called trial, nor how the high king could be so easily manipulated. She'd been targeted, and he wasn't going to consider for one minute that there could be deception at play. *The truth doesn't change just because they don't believe me,* she thought angrily. One or many of the fae were out to get her, but why? None of them would even listen to the facts. She continued taking mouthfuls of berries, her raging questions going unanswered.

A noise at the door surprised her, and she nearly knocked over her glass of water in her haste to look up. In walked Judicaël in all his shocking, mystifying beauty. It wafted from him like an alluring scent, trying to beguile anyone in its path.

The door shut on its own behind him as he stepped closer to her, and her level of discomfort grew with each stride. He stared at her like a person trying to decide if he was hungry enough to eat the meal laid out before him. He stopped just in front of her and kicked the tray off to the side. She couldn't help but cringe as the last of her food scattered across the floor. He reclaimed her attention when he lifted her by the shackles without laying a finger on her. Though she could still painfully feel them around her wrists, she was relieved to be able to sit upright without the pressing weight. Judicaël slowly crouched so they were at eye level. Catherine inhaled deeply and waited, watching him watch her.

At last, he spoke. "Your magic is like nothing I've seen in a druid."

"That's because I'm not a real druid."

Through narrowed eyes he examined her. "Yes, your magic wasn't learned but given. I see that now."

What had he been seeing before?

He continued. "Still, you fascinate me." He nimbly stood and waved a hand over her shackles. They let go of her skin completely but stayed afloat in the air and remained to hover closely around her wrist. Then he walked in a slow, deliberate manner around the room, casually inspecting it while also somehow avoiding the spilled food with each step. "I wonder, what do you know of my realm?"

"Nothing of fact, only tales," Catherine said, discreetly trying to unlatch or pull off the shackles. Her small palm flame fizzled out every time.

"Would you like to learn? Stay by my side as my mate, and you will learn everything there is to know."

What? Catherine halted mid-action. Had she heard correctly? "Forgive me, but however much I've been interested in the mysteries of your realm in the past, I no longer care. Free me. Let me find my family and leave."

Judicaël was frozen still, gazing out the window, enraptured by the night sky. He looked like something out of a painting. Catherine watched him, but her mind was back on her task. She worked without making a sound and with barely noticeable movement. Finally, a flame quietly flared. She used her fingers to sculpt and mold it into a tool that would cut through her shackles.

"None of the fae hold my interest in this way, but you, you intrigue me. It's strange, I have never found humans to be of any value other than for their energy. Until now."

Eyes set on him, she carved her fire tool in and burned past the top layer with ease. "From mere interest you offer marriage?"

"I would if it were only that, yes," he replied, his gaze still fixed on the sky. "Nevertheless, no, I also hunger for you. Or something about you. I can't place it yet, but I will in due time." Catherine felt a sudden rush of awkwardness and dread flow through her body. "I offer a place next to my throne, where you'll fill my curiosity until your death, which will be dramatically delayed should you accept."

Blinking a few extra times, she tried to register his words, and when she did, she gawked at him behind his back. If she could, she'd run screaming from his offer even if it'd been for eternal youth. "I am already married, and even if I weren't, I'd want nothing to do with you or your throne."

Judicaël turned around with a glare a few seconds after Catherine snuffed out the sculpted flame, which had just cut through the last of her binds. "Then you'll die here," he said.

Catherine's eyes challenged his. "If I die, I'll die taking your realm with me."

He raised an eyebrow while curiously looking over the length of her weakened body. "Doubtful."

She set her jaw and glowered at him. He didn't appear to mind. In fact, he tilted his head slightly and stared at her with intrigue as he came over to invade her space once more.

He was close enough now. This was her chance. Catherine wrenched her hands out of the floating shackles, and the unlatched chains fell to the floor with a clatter. Flames burst out of her palms in front of her, but Judicaël stepped agilely aside. It wouldn't have mattered if he hadn't because the flames died out almost instantly after licking at her already sore wrists with the ends of their burning tongues. She let out a restrained scream and stumbled back against the nearest wall.

Cool and casual, Judicaël stayed perfectly still. "It seems whatever has been draining you has finally taken all of your magic. Next will be your life. Are you prepared to die?"

What was happening? Her fire had never burned her before. "I'm stronger than you think," she muttered, carefully cradling her hands against her chest.

"A human's strength is nothing in this world. Only your energy has worth."

"You're wrong," she said, but he was already walking away.

At the door, he spoke without turning to meet her eyes. "My offer will remain."

"If I don't accept?"

"Then this room is where you shall die."

She watched the glass door shut behind him and then turn into a mirror once more. Her reflection was pitiful, ghostly as if she were already dead. His offer was insulting in every possible way, but what concerned her more was the pain she'd just felt from her own fire. Still, she was one step closer to escape. Either he'd forgotten her broken shackles, or having seen how weakened she was, he wasn't concerned about them. *It doesn't matter what Judicaël thinks. Focus.* She set on the task of healing her wrists. Maybe after a rest she could summon enough healing fire to do the trick. If not, she would have to fight her way out without it.

The wall she was propped up against began to shift, and as stars greeted her with twinkles and winks, she was almost lulled to sleep. She slumped down where she sat and looked below, ignoring the squashed berries. The floor shifted, and she could see more of the glass castle underneath her room. There were staircases upon staircases, and hallways upon hallways, with adjacent rooms and the occasional mirror within. Tree trunks and branches weaved throughout, and every level and layer of glass was a strange and confusing labyrinth.

Whereas her level was mostly barren of life, on others, faeries sauntered to and fro, solo or in pairs. Soldiers and guards lined a few deeper levels, where articles in the armories glimmered in the moon's touch. Had any looked up and wondered about her? Trying to make sense of the sight, Catherine grew more tired. Her eyes ached, and her eyelids kept falling over them. *Maybe I should move to the bed of leaves.* Her lethargic legs felt like two heavy boulders keeping her trapped.

She felt trapped in every sense of the word.

"Catherine."

Her head bobbed and rolled until her chin hung at her chest.

"Catherine, wake up."

In her dreamless sleep, she had the vague sense someone was calling her. Then the room was silent. Too silent. Stinging pain resonated through her wrist wounds. All at once she bolted awake against the wall, arms propping her up beneath her seat. Catherine glanced down at them. The burns were still there. She slumped slowly down again and tried to relax her shoulders. She was still in her glass prison.

She let her head roll to one shoulder, looking over her side and found herself nose to nose with another face. *"How can you sleep in this place?"*

Catherine jumped away.

"Shh, shh, it's me."

With a moan, she exhaled loudly, and slowly returned to where he rested. She desperately wanted to believe it was him, that they were actually together right now, and it wasn't all in her head. "Bowen?" He was see-through, and when the castle's glass walls shifted again, she almost lost him in the night sky. "You're a ghost!" she cried.

"Yes," he said, and she could feel her hopes fading. Then his eyes widened. *"No, I'm not dead!"*

"You're still alive?" She could barely whisper.

"Yes, my love. You saved me from Gwenaël, remember?"

Catherine sighed in relief. It hadn't all been an illusion. "Thank God." She gulped back the tears that threatened. "What happened to you after I freed you? Why are you still bodiless?"

"I don't know. My body disappeared when the mirror broke. After they took you, I followed them to stay close."

What? "You've been with me all this time and didn't say anything until now?"

He shook his head. *"No, often something takes over me, and I can't see or hear anything until it passes. Then I have to search for you all over again."*

"How long do you think? How long until—"

"I don't know. I think when my body goes I'll go for good. Or the other way around."

Catherine swallowed her sadness and rolled her lips. He was

here now. She didn't want to spend this precious time in despair. Bowen tilted his head, and his longer curls fell in front of her eyes. She reached to move them as she normally did, but her hand went straight through him. He was just air. He smiled and gazed at her. Oh, how she wished she could wrap her arms around him, or grab hold of his hands, at least. Instead, they sat together in lover's silence, telling each other a thousand things in one look.

He broke the silence. *"What happened to your hair?"*

"It fell out because of these," she said, pulling off the scarf and tracing some of the black lines with her finger. Bowen quietly examined them. "Do you know what they are?"

"I think they're a protection spell. Did you say one before they appeared?"

Catherine tried to remember if she'd said anything accidentally. "No, nothing." She shrugged.

"Your body is always in self-preservation mode on its own. I think as soon as it sensed an attack, it acted."

"Gwenaël suggested they're why I kept my magic for as long as I did."

"Doubtless." Bowen shook his head, and his ghostly curls flopped over themselves.

She glanced downward, feeling the worry overrun her face. "And Judicaël—"

"Never mind what Judicaël said. I don't think your magic is gone yet."

"I don't know what I think." Catherine sighed. "I can't feel it, Bowen. Not like before."

He looked at her in silence for a moment as he rubbed his smooth chin. *"Is there still a small glint somewhere in your mind? Anything at all?"*

She thought a moment before nodding. Sure. Somewhere.

"It may be that you have to work harder to summon it, but as long as those lines are there, your magic still resides."

"What if I can't summon it?" She bit her lower lip in frustration. Bowen didn't answer, just watched her with that knowing look. She took some deliberate breaths to calm herself. "Okay then, somehow I will. Until it's all gone," she grumbled. "However soon that is, I guess." Without her magic, she couldn't hope to fight the opposing magic trying to take every last ounce of hers. Catherine shivered and wrapped her arms around herself. There was no giving up. Giving up meant certain death. She had to find out who or what was doing this to her.

Bowen moved in front of her and wrapped his arms above her own. The gesture didn't provide the usual warmth. Instead, it added to the cold on her goosebump-covered skin. Despite this, she loved knowing he was there, and that she was engulfed in his actual spirit. Though she wished that in her earlier frantic state that she'd put on thick pants instead of a fanning skirt.

"I'm afraid," Bowen whispered in her ear.

Catherine pulled back to meet his eyes and saw in them the fear he spoke of. He had always been her pillar of strength and wisdom. His many years hadn't worn his virtue down. Rather, they'd given him confidence that draped over his broad and noble figure like a royal robe. She raised her eyebrows in surprise. "Of what?"

"Dying. I've been alive for so long, and I've longed for death's release for most of that time. But now that death is almost here, I don't want to go yet."

"Yet? Will there be a time when you'll want to go?"

"Yes, right after you. Only then can my soul rest. It won't as long as I know you're still here and in danger."

Catherine couldn't let herself dwell on his words. If she did, that might somehow make them happen sooner, and she wouldn't give the words power like that. "I'm going to find a way out of here, Bowen," she said quietly.

Suddenly he stiffened. *"Shh, someone's coming."*

10

Before Catherine could register what Bowen had said, the door opened, and Loïc appeared at the threshold. He didn't say anything, just looked at her down his pointed nose disdainfully. Their heavy stares locked in a silent battle, in a timeless world. His eyes seemed hateful as ever, revealing murderous thoughts.

"Judicaël will suspect you," she said.

Loïc gave a short smug laugh but didn't move.

Catherine pushed herself to her feet. As she did, she noticed her lover's ghostly limbs, which had been wrapped around her so recently, had vanished. Quickly scanning the room, she saw that Bowen's spirit was nowhere to be found. Her heart fell, but her gaze climbed up and set itself on the imposing fae. If that had been her last moment with her husband, she wasn't going to forget the interruption that had ended it.

"Get out of here." Any leftover fear hiding in the dark crevices of her broken heart had been driven away. "I mean it. Get out!"

"Curiosity doesn't snap and bite at you?"

Just hearing him speak made her fists ball up. She didn't have the faintest idea what he was talking about, but frankly, she didn't care. She wanted more than anything to burn him to a crisp in the doorway. "I don't want to hear anything you have to say. You are nothing but a cowardly snake, and cowardice disgusts me almost as much as pitiful arrogance."

Loïc's eyes narrowed, and his lips curled into a snarl. "I am a fae king. You are a mere human woman."

"And you are a dishonorable lunatic underestimating his enemies. A human woman is stronger than you think, but I'm not just any human. I'm not one of the hundreds kidnapped by the fae over the centuries."

"Why should I be afraid of you, a hideous thing? It's appalling he offered you anything."

How did he know about Judicaël's offer? She ignored him and continued. "You should be afraid. Not of me but of what will come because of your own actions. This is what will hunt you down, and it will be far worse than anything I could ever do to you. And I could hurt you more than you realize."

"Without your power you're nothing."

She wouldn't let him get away with that. "No, without it I'm still a woman with flaws and people I love, who love me back, that make me what I am: strong. With your power, you are still nothing."

"Then after your power is gone, and I make sure all your loves cease to exist, all you'll be left with is your flaws." He smiled. A toothy and frightening smile. "Right before you die."

Catherine knew he was crazy, jealous of someone he deemed weaker than himself, but his unrelenting words roused that small seed of doubt in her. "I mean it," she yelled. "Get out of here!" Her words echoed off the glass walls.

"I don't take orders from anyone," he said, sneering again.

"Wrong." Judicaël's voice rang out from behind Loïc, who quickly spun around. "All that you have is mine, and if you wish to keep it, you will mind your tongue."

Loïc sank a foot in height, changing his body language from

savage to submissive in an instant. Respectfully he bowed his head. "My king."

Judicaël eyed him suspiciously. "Why are you here? I told you she was mine."

"I suspected she would try to escape, my king."

"I am no fool, Loïc," the high king said, staring him down.

Loïc remained in a humble position but continued to speak. "She's bewitched you. I was going to save you the trouble of watching her die."

"The next time you defy me will be the last."

Loïc's eyes widened briefly before Judicaël waved for him to leave. Disgraced, the fae hobbled out of the room like a bird with a crippled wing.

Catherine met Judicaël's gaze. His intense eyes were still enraged, and she noticed that the glow always radiating from his body brightened when he was furious. "Did he harm you?"

Though she was thankful his appearance had saved her from Loïc, seeing his face was almost as unsettling. "No," she said plainly.

His gazed calmed, and so did his white glow. "Come with me," he said, his voice softening.

After a moment's hesitation, she followed him out of the room and down a different hall than before. It led to a gaping dark hole running through and separating them from the rest of the glass floor. A wide bridge arched over it, and despite her fear, she couldn't help but peek over the railing as they crossed to see anything that might explain an abyss beneath the castle.

"It is a closed-off realm," he said over his shoulder. "We were locked out for disobeying long ago, so I built all of my castles on top to spite them."

Them? Catherine thought, curious about the history. Due to the slightly stronger light now glimmering off the high king, she decided not to risk questioning him.

Soon, they stepped off the bridge to arrive in the grand throne room that had served as her courtroom hours before. It was deathly silent now, completely emptied of fae. The walls phased out to reveal a receding dark blue sky tinted with purple. The moon had gone, and the remaining stars were winking their goodbyes. Dawn was near.

Judicaël moved to the throne and sat while Catherine continued to gaze at the sky, sending her love back to the stars. After a few moments, she began to feel self-conscious and turned to the throne. He was watching her. *If he's waiting for me to speak first, he'll be waiting a long time,* she thought stubbornly. Before she could run through the possible reasons he had brought her back there, he shifted and then stood.

She moved backward as he approached. "I thought you might have given more consideration to my offer?"

"No, I won't ever consider it," she said firmly with her head held high. "You had my answer the minute you left last time."

His eyes narrowed. "Your life could be lengthened by two, maybe three lifetimes. How can you dash my offer aside so carelessly?" Catherine cursed as she backed into the wall. "I can return to you your beauty, your vigor. Everything you're losing." He stopped directly in front of her, and she was forced to look up at his towering figure. His shoulders were broad, and his loose garments had been pushed aside to reveal his lean, muscled torso. Clearly, he was a beautiful and powerful fae. He was the high king. She struggled to understand why he wouldn't pick someone else to give such an offer to, someone who would actually want it. He caught her gaze. "Is my shape pleasing to you?"

Catherine ignored him. "Can you return Bella and my husband to me? Because that's all I want."

His brow furrowed in puzzlement but then smoothed as he lifted his slender hand and caressed her cheek.

She batted it away. "Don't touch me."

Judicaël rolled his eyes closed as he inhaled deeply. "Ah, that scent of yours is enticing." He caught her gaze again. "For a millennium I've waited for such a fragrance, one that could still my soul. Therefore, I'll ask once more. Will you be mine?"

Her mouth twisted into a grimace. "Wait another millennium, and I'll still be cringing in my grave at the thought."

"You are strange, druid woman. My throne, all but one of the realms at your call, and yet you refuse. Nothing tempts you to my side?"

She set her jaw and looked away from him, but he leaned in, and despite her efforts to push him away, his lips met hers. She bit his lip, and he pulled back. "Stop it," she spat. A look of staggering confusion spread across his face as she pushed him backward.

He'd stolen a kiss from her. It wasn't his to take. It was Bowen's, only ever Bowen's, and now her husband's lips wouldn't be the last ones on hers. Judicaël had unwittingly ripped that lover's solace from her. Her heart was on fire, and tears burned her cheeks on the way down. "I'll never be yours, so just stop trying." She tasted blood in her mouth. "If you don't, then I'll—"

"What shall you do?" His fierce glow illuminated the whole room.

"I'll tear down your realm, starting with this castle," she said, her wild emotions swelling.

Something was bubbling inside her, itching to get out. A familiar heat, strong and deliberate, was returning. She could feel the fire wrapping its coils around each of her bones then seeping through and out, ready to unleash powerful flames at her call. Though she could feel the heat burning her again, it didn't hurt or leave a mark this time. Instead, the sensation was almost pleasant.

"Without me, you're nearly dead standing there," he said, oblivious to her growing flames. "How shall you?"

"Burn it!" Catherine screamed and stretched out her arms. A flame shot out from inside her elbow, looped around it like a bow, and met with a long flame arrow that had burst from the palm of her opposite arm's hand. She aimed and let it fly.

For the first time, the high king showed signs of humanity in his bewildered face.

The throne caught fire. She spun around and released another arrow-shaped flame, and the bridge over the deep crevice was set ablaze. She didn't wait for Judicaël to recover from his stunned state, stalking across the fiery bridge before it collapsed, falling into the darkness below.

Taking off at a run, she followed the rising sunlight shooting shades of color across each glass surface and through the air. No one chased her, and no one appeared out of empty space to stop her, but she didn't dare slow her pace. She weaved through the castle maze as fast as she could.

Passing an armory, she stopped just as the glass walls went transparent and showed her she'd gone below the earth to one of the deeper levels. Luckily, it was just up one level that she needed, and she made it to the top of the stairs where she happened to recognize the place just outside the castle walls. The courtyard of lakes.

There had to be a door or window somewhere. As she searched, she kept expecting to find a faerie guard or catch a glimpse of one of the nobility from her trial down every hall and every bend. To her astonishment, she never did. The in-between mode became visible in the light, and something caught her eye. The stencils of the seasons, each cut out against the view. She'd seen gales, snowflakes, icicles and more decorating the borders of every hallway and circling over the major entrances such as the armory, while autumn and the other seasons didn't appear to do anything other than fill in the rest of the glass. After much confusion from the illusion of the glass, she had a hunch the dominating season would lead her out. She followed it for a time, growing more excited with each step, and her excitement peaked when she spotted the outside wall spying on the lakes up ahead. She fought with a couple of glass doors, fingers slipping until at last she pried them open and was free.

Outside on the forest floor, her feet found warmth and comfort, and she hurried along by the side of the castle. Though she was panting from the exertion, she knew her heart raced because of the freedom flowing through her veins and filling her lungs; the scent was delicious. Eventually she came to the place of many lakes, where the sun also reflected on the waters and shimmered with rainbows of color, each beam bouncing off of the prism castle.

Catherine stopped dead in her tracks and then ran back just far enough to run her hand over a glass wall that stood between four large trees. Their branches wove high in and out of the castle and castle grounds. She closed her eyes tightly and placed her hand on the glass directly across from her chest. Still panting, she quickly regained focus and summoned her waning magic. She could feel the black pattern on her head burning, but it no longer caused her pain. Sounds of scuffling from deep within the castle fell on her ears. Her eyes snapped open, and she focused every ounce of energy on a single thought.

SHATTER.

Catherine turned on her heel and fled past the lakes, past the trees, and deep into the southern fae forests. Far past the danger point, she turned around and released her mental rope. Within seconds, she heard a fracturing sound like no other. Billions of little lights flashed, and their reflections leaped, dived, and skidded over each, surrounding the castle in a flurry of chaos. Glass crumbled away from the trees, and then, starting at the highest level, the castle plunged to the ground.

11

THE SUN WAS high before Catherine took a moment to sit and rest her overworked legs. She'd finally put enough distance between herself and the castle. She didn't think the fae knew her whereabouts or they would have recaptured her by now, considering how much magic she'd just expended. She hadn't wanted to lag and risk giving them a chance to find her. While on the run through one of the vast surrounding woods, she'd called out to Bowen, but he'd made no appearance. To avoid breaking down, she thought about her magic. Where had the sudden burst of energy sprung from? She guessed the unstable shift in her magic had something to do with whatever was draining and manipulating her power, but of course, she couldn't be sure of anything.

Frustration and despair seemed to be normal aspects of her existence now. Catherine felt chained to the will of her body, and every day those chains grew heavier. She'd assumed the end wasn't far off, and then her power had come back when she truly needed it. *Nothing is ever certain,* she thought. That was why she couldn't give up hope.

Feeling her pulse slow to a comfortable rhythm, she closed her eyes and tried reaching out with her other senses. The sun's healing rays warmed and caressed her bruises with comforting fingers. Though they fed her bones, her hunger was less than sated. She distracted herself with questions. Was the black pattern lining her head still working? Bowen's words repeated in her mind. Was it possible it was also protecting him through their oathing bond? How long would the mark last? She knew she couldn't keep up with whatever or whoever was draining her magic.

"Are you there?" Her voice was barely a whisper. *Bowen.* She squeezed her hand above her heart, wishing for a clue, any clue at all that his spirit was still drifting, still with her.

Nothing came. Sweat trickled over her brow and down her neck. The sun fueled parts of her but, in her weakened state, drained others. Her throat was sore and scratchy, and the sun aided the dry air following her every move. There was little shade in the area. Not to mention her recent aerobic workout alone had given her ample reason to thirst for a flash flood.

Catherine stretched her blistered feet, wishing she had thought to put on shoes. She knew full well that in the frantic state of mind she'd been in, she couldn't possibly have hoped to be that resourceful. When she'd gotten a few good stretches in, she decided to hunt for water. There had to be a river, lake, or even a creek somewhere nearby. Then, taking another hard look at the rickety trees and the dry soil from which they'd sprung, she wondered if she'd actually end up dying of thirst before anything else.

She walked for a long time in one direction and found nothing. She turned in another direction and found nothing. She became more and more downtrodden by nature's cruel ways. Her body screamed at her. Her throat was so sore it burned, and her mouth was too dry to help her cracked, bleeding lips. She took off her scarf to pat her face and neck often.

And then, a beautiful sound filled her ears. Running water. Her mind was instantly alert. The dry grass crunched loudly under her feet as she followed the sound, but there was nothing to be found. Had she imagined it into being? Just when she was about to fall on the ground and give in to her overwhelming thirst, another sound brought her to a stop.

A soft melody suddenly filled the air like an intoxicating perfume. Catherine could feel its intention was to allure, persuade, and to capture. It sounded different from Loïc's music. The magic of this melody was stronger but did not affect her mind or senses, even in her weakened state. Suddenly, a masculine fae appeared from thin air, a golden cloak and hood covering his identifying features. She managed to take a few wobbly paces back and tried to focus, but her energy had depleted too far for any hope of rapt comprehension.

Before her eyes closed on her, she saw a pale hand reach out. Her legs gave out, but her heavy eyelids somehow pulled themselves back again. Golden fabric glimmered in the sun. The fae threw back the hood of his cloak, and she drew back with a gasp.

"No, I am not your enemy," he said, his tone urgent.

"Like hell you're not!"

Alarm spread through her as he grabbed hold of her arms, firm but gentle. "I'm not the high king!" She froze. "My name is Cadeyrn," he said, more softly.

Cadeyrn. That name. She'd heard it spoken in the court. Loïc's face always twisted at the mere mention of it. Catherine relaxed her shoulders and stopped struggling. The fae let go of her but didn't withdraw. She eyed him cautiously. Though his voice was different, soothing, she was unwilling to trust any fae completely.

"Your eyes have that dreadful look," he said. "I see you've met Loïc . . . and Judicaël."

Catherine nodded, and her caution turned to wonder. Cadeyrn looked almost exactly like Judicaël, except his hair stopped at the middle of his back and his eyes, though also a steely gray, suggested a gentle soul rather than a fierce king.

"Will my appearance stun you from speech for long?" He raised an eyebrow. He was also more human-looking than Judicaël, and this gave Catherine a sense of comfort.

She blinked out her astonishment and swallowed back the remainder of the fight in her. "Sorry, I was scared for my freedom," she said. "And my life."

"As you should be. He seeks you still."

A sudden thought filled her with horror. "Are you going to turn me back over to him?"

"No."

Catherine couldn't hide how relieved she was to hear that one word.

"No one escapes him unless he lets them. He enjoys the hunt."

Her shoulders tensed again. It was the first time she realized that Judicaël hadn't fought back like Gwenaël had. He was certainly capable, being the high king of the fae. Cadeyrn was right.

The fae walked to the nearest tree and leaned his back against it, crossing his arms and legs in front of him. "I have no desire to add strength to a bridge used by fools and deceivers."

Catherine waited for him to continue, but after a long pause, she felt her thirst raging once more. She glanced around, trying to determine where the sound was coming from.

"The creek is near."

She spun around to look at him. "How did you—"

"It is obvious thirst consumes you. Come with me," he said curtly and led the way.

When they reached the bubbling brook in no time at all, Catherine fell to her knees and plunged in both of her arms up to her shoulders before dunking her head. The cool, crisp water lapped and rolled over her skin, leaving her breathless. She drank and splashed to her full delight, and when she was satisfied, she lay back on the ground, letting herself slowly sink into the soft earth.

She could feel him looking her over with a curious eye, taking in her torn clothing and gaunt appearance. "I knew you before they found you. It was a fae of my kingdom who made the deal with you, after which they brought their prize to me as penance for another disobedient act." She briefly remembered the eerie, childlike fae she first met the year before, at the time never imagining that taking a lock of her hair could be a crime. Catherine rolled her gaze over to Cadeyrn. A deep, melodious note fell with each syllable he uttered. It was a struggle to pay attention to his words and not his strange yet alluring voice.

"Though I cannot fathom where it comes from, or how that much magic is within you, your lock of hair is quite powerful. Any fae could see it with a mere glance." One of Cadeyrn's eyebrows twitched above his unblinking stare. "I hid it away and told no one, but somehow word still spread. It was the last strike. The one that broke the kingdoms apart."

He didn't ask any questions, and Catherine didn't volunteer any answers. Besides, she had no idea the extent of the magic within her. "I heard. Aside from me, they also accuse you of treason and blame you for this war. They said you want to overthrow Judicaël."

"I don't want any such thing. There is treason here, but it does not come from my hands. Judicaël has been deceived by one or many in his court."

Catherine slowly rose up and leaned heavily on one hand. "Why weren't you there to defend yourself?"

"Civil battles north of here blocked my attendance. I suspect that was the very purpose of the battle."

"To keep you out so you couldn't defend yourself."

He nodded. "I'm sorry you were taken prisoner. It was a play to aid their condemning me." His perfect brow suddenly wrinkled. "But to be fair, it wouldn't have happened if you hadn't come here. Why did you enter our realm? They wouldn't have found you otherwise."

Her bright red blood on the white sheets with Bowen's stricken body lying on top suddenly flashed before her eyes, and she swallowed hard. "The last thing I wanted was to come back here, to see any more of your secret world, but I had to. The fae kidnapped my friend, and stole my stone."

Cadeyrn looked away, his stern gaze rife with thought. "They were watching you."

Catherine exhaled loudly as she shifted her weight to sit up evenly and cross her legs. His words made sense. Someone had to have been. Maybe Loïc, maybe Gwenaël. Just how long had she been under surveillance? Perhaps they'd even been watching her before she ventured into their realm the first time. "But why? Is my power really that threatening just because it makes me an equal to some of you?"

The fae laced graceful fingers through silky hair, which fell from them just as gracefully. "I sense they found a way to take your power and lured you here to keep it." She gaped at his words. It unsettled her to think that a devious fae had been stalking her for any length of time, but especially to think it was recent and possibly constant to put some spell on her without her notice. They may have even been present at her private wedding ceremony. She just looked at Cadeyrn, too overwhelmed to reply. He'd been watching her right back the whole time that her thoughts surged.

"Sleep," he said.

She was startled out of her minor stupor. "What?"

"If they come, I will hide you. You need your rest to keep your magic."

Catherine shook her head. "I can't, I don't have time. If I sleep, the two people I'm fighting for might die as I dream. If they're not already gone."

"As you will." Cadeyrn's face was untroubled again, the very picture of calm as he relaxed against the tree. His presence was so different from his doppelgänger's, and Catherine couldn't help but look at him curiously again. Where Judicaël was the harsh, fickle storm, Cadeyrn was the light sprinkle that mated with the all-comforting breeze.

As she examined his features, the strange music living inside him made itself heard again but stayed at a low volume, as if trying to lull her to sleep. Catherine shrugged herself out of it. She needed to find out whatever she could from this king and then be on her way, not nap and allow him the opportunity to take her somewhere for however long. She still didn't know if she could trust him completely.

"What started the civil war?" she asked, trying to distract him. "It couldn't have been just my power that tipped everything over, could it?" Even while she said it, she considered that it might be true. Bowen had once told her how much they used to heavily rely on the ancient druids' energy. Perhaps their supply was compromised after all this time. She had no way of knowing based on her own interactions with them. She'd only met kings and queens who all seemed powerful enough. She had overtaken each of them though, even with how weak she was.

"Civil battle begins with uncivil thoughts, and is usually led by selfish decisions, gathering the fooled and the ignorant," he said cryptically, without turning her way.

"But do you die?" she asked timidly. He slowly nodded. "I got the impression you were immortal," she mumbled.

"We are."

"I don't understand."

"We can be killed, but we do not naturally die."

"So the civil war is very real." She looked down at her clasped hands in her lap.

"Brutally."

She stood. She'd made a decision. "Thank you for your kindness, King. I won't forget it."

"Tread with caution." Cadeyrn's glossy orbs were filled with concern and flecked with warning. "You don't yet know of all kinds of fae, and there are those who prefer to move outside the physical. Some retain the most power in their spirit form." He paused. "Though you carry immense and unpredictable power in your blood, it being drained as it is, your time is undeniably fleeting."

Catherine furrowed her brow and nodded, keeping his gaze. She had to survive this, she just had to. "And what will you do, with everyone but your subjects against you?"

"I will end this war, one way or another."

She bid the pleasant fae king goodbye. It was time to continue on her way, whichever way that was. His music faded into the air behind her until all was silent once more. Before long, she was scolding herself. Why hadn't she asked him for help? *He probably doesn't have the time to spare,* she thought. He was fighting a war, after all.

And so was she.

Catherine didn't want to fight anymore. Her soul was exhausted, but she would fight to the very end for those she loved, whatever the cost.

12

Bella fell on her scraped and bleeding knees for what seemed like the hundredth time. Somehow, Danny had found the endurance to keep picking her right back up again. The foreboding vibes spearing the air suggested that they would vanish altogether if they let their guard down for even a moment. He knew they had to push on.

Suddenly Danny tripped over a protruding tree root and fell face-first. Scrambling to his knees, he punched fistfuls of dirt into the soft earth, cursing under his breath. He hated this. He was either not strong enough, or he kept making mistakes. Stupidly tripping fell under the last category.

"Dan." He turned at the sound of Bella's wobbly voice. She was squeezing her stomach, probably feeling the same overwhelming nausea as he was. "Are you hurt?"

He shrugged his shoulders violently before slamming the dirt with another swift blow. So much time he'd wasted in life autoplayed in his brain. He felt like every recent good intention turned into a stupid move, as though there was preconceived plotting out to get him, just to make an elaborate and humiliating show of how much of a waste he was.

"It was bound to happen because of my hair, if not the forest," Bella remarked.

"It is shocking it took me this long," he said hatefully, still hunched over, looking at the ground. He tried to regain his breath.

"Please, get up," she said quietly, her voice crestfallen.

Danny clenched his hands and gripped the dirt. He hated hearing Bella sound like that, he hated how weak she was feeling, he hated everything that was happening. He was the weak one, with nothing to offer that would save her or his sister, wherever she was. They could keep running, but where to? As far as he could tell, the forest was endless.

"Get up," she repeated.

"Why?" he grumbled. "I can't save us, so what's the point?"

"Because, I—" She stopped mid-sentence and he shot up in alarm, catching her just before she hit the ground.

He wrapped his arms around her and leaned his forehead against hers, wishing he could erase all her struggles with a single embrace.

"I'm still alive," she whispered. "You're still saving me."

"Stay awake," he urged.

"See?" She nodded, closing her eyes.

"Don't do that, come on." He shook her, and her eyes rolled open.

"Kiss me again, true love and all." The corners of her lips perked up into a laughing smile.

"You still don't believe?" He raised an eyebrow. "That freak you were going out with wouldn't have been able to save you this way. You didn't love him, right?" Bella shook her head slightly and furrowed her brow, and despite all their troubles, Danny felt his mouth spread into a wide, shining smile.

"Kiss," she whispered, and he leaned in to grant her another breath of strength. Pulling away, he smiled down at her and slowly caressed her cheeks with his fingers.

"As much as I like doing that, I wish this power were stronger."

Bella returned his weak smile. "Me too. It's taking both of us to ward off this sleep-trapping spell, and I don't have much strength."

"I'm growing weaker too." He helped her to her feet. "Just a sec," he said, releasing her.

Bella's eyes grew wider. "What is it?"

He waved off her concern. "Nothing. I'm just gonna walk ahead. Try to see if I can find any indication of the right direction out of here."

Her eyes calmed, but she nodded reluctantly before she started to gather up her long hair in her arms, flinching with every snag and pull.

Gently holding onto Bella's hair as their lifeline, Danny walked down what seemed like an actual path. It was the clearest route he'd found so far. Though hunger threatened to overtake him, his vision seemed to be getting sharper. *Weird,* he thought. He felt like an owl.

Rounding a cluster of thin trees with barely any leaves remaining on their spindly limbs, he thought he saw someone ahead. He ducked down behind some bushes but bobbed his head out just far enough to get a look. *Ouch!* His hand scraped against a thorny part of one bush, and he dropped the golden locks beside him to inspect it. He pulled out the sticking thorn and brought his hand to his mouth, sucking on the tiny wound as he looked back out at the mystery person or creature. Was it one of the fae? The figure was still too far away for him to tell. He waited, but soon determined the figure wasn't coming toward him as it disappeared.

Danny pushed himself upright, breathing a small sigh of relief. It was probably for the best. He didn't want to risk asking for help from any fae. Beneath his shoes, fallen twigs and leaves snapped and crunched as he followed the path back the way he came. After a few minutes of walking, sudden panic rose to his throat. This couldn't be the way he'd come. He'd forgotten to pick Bella's hair back up. Too panicked to throw a fit, he tried to rush back to the bush he'd ducked behind. Nothing was there. Maybe it was a different bush. He went to another that looked familiar, but nothing. He did this two more times before he resolved to just follow back as best he could. It was taking too long to get back to Bella though. He should have reached her by now. His eyes bugged out as he strained to recognize something, anything that would help him find his way back to her. "Bella!" His voice wafted through the air like vapor, echoing into the gloom.

He fell to his knees and belted out a cry of despair. He shouldn't have left her side. He cursed himself for letting go of her hair for even a second. Images of her being recaptured, or trapped in a deathly slumber, wouldn't stop revolving in his mind. Now he was completely lost, and because of him, Bella and her magic hair were nowhere to be found.

Catherine's ankle had begun to bleed again, but she walked on. Did it keep reopening because her magic lost strength as her body did? She slowly became aware of thousands of glittering lights not belonging to the sky. They were everywhere. Some were perfectly still, others moved slowly, and the rest skittered wildly in every direction as if their purpose was to fill every untouched spot.

Catherine found herself looking for prisms along the forest floor, but there was nothing but plain soil.

From her encounters so far, she half expected to hear music, but there was no sound other than the increasing beat of her heart and her untamable breathing. The lights seemed to have individual personalities. They reminded her of eyes. Her forearms prickled as she pushed on, hoping they wouldn't follow her. With a shudder, she thought of eyes in portraits of people long dead.

Silence grew and overwhelmed the space, then all the lights shifted, and Catherine nearly jumped out of her skin. They pulsed inward once before skittering in separate directions. She stopped in her tracks. They moved inward again but not together this time. Instead, they were like swarming insects, coming closer and closer until they covered her. She felt them. They weren't merely light, but something that could push and prod. Tiny voices whispered close to her ears, and then she knew: *Some retain the most power in their spirit form.* Cadeyrn's words echoed in her mind. Thousands of fae were consuming her energy.

Frantically, she swiped and scraped to free herself, but more moved inward from the trees and accumulated on her skin and clothes. The pressure kept her from inhaling enough oxygen, and her chest started to burn and ache. All she could think was, *trapped!*

A loud and sudden BOOM sounded in the distance, and Catherine gasped and gulped for air as the thousands of lights scurried off toward it. She grabbed her throat with one hand and squeezed the other against her middle. The black spots in her vision began to fade, but she couldn't think about anything other than breathing.

The next thing she knew she was tumbling to the forest floor. Rough leaves clung to her arms and legs. Quickly rolling back to her feet but staying low, she met the gaze of the caramel-brown eyes directly in front of her.

"Danny," she said on an exhale. Her dreadful thirst had already been quenched. This couldn't be a mirage, could it?

From his crouched position, he leaped forward and embraced her tightly. "I found you, I found you," he repeated over and over again.

She squeezed her arms around his middle, relieved to see him again. Then worry rose higher inside her stormy stomach. She'd never seen her brother so worn and pale, and she'd seen him through some bad times. "What are you doing here?" she said, pulling away just enough to see his face. "Don't you know the fae could do anything they wanted with you?"

"I remember you saying that." He leaned back and plopped to the ground.

"Then what the hell are you in here for?"

"I came after you and Bella."

Though irritated that he'd followed her into such a dangerous place, Catherine felt a jolt of hope in her heart. "And?"

"I found her," he said. Her heart started to swell, but the relief was short-lived. "And I literally just lost her again. I was trying to find out if you took her—well, not you. I thought you were a fae."

She wanted to cry. Bella was still lost and now her brother was in the middle of this nightmare. "How long have you been in here?"

"I couldn't tell ya." He frowned. "I do know I'm starving to death though, and maybe you're just an illusion. Maybe all of this is in my head, and I'm actually still lying where I passed out before," he said, waving his hands around wildly.

Right, Catherine thought. She always forgot that time was different here than in the human realm. Days as she knew them could have passed. Or weeks. She wouldn't know how long this place had been her cage until she left it. If she left it.

"I'm not an apparition, Danny. Listen, can you remember how long I'd been gone before you came after me?"

"A few hours I think, but I don't know."

"And how did you find Bella?"

"She was standing somewhere in the middle of the woods frozen still, a collection item for a sadistic fae," he said with disgust. "I managed to trick him and free her, but it's not permanent. The spell he put on her isn't broken, and now I may never find her again." He shoved his face in his hands.

"Danny, stop it! I can't do this if you fall apart on me because then I'll fall apart." She swallowed her rising panic. It killed her that she'd been so close to finding her friend. Just a few seconds earlier and maybe she would have.

Danny sobbed quietly into his hands a moment before smearing the salty tears across his face and up through his long bangs. He looked at her, his eyes red and swollen. This must not have been the first time he'd cried out here. What was the next move? She had to get her bearings, but something about Danny's story kept nagging at her. "Did the fae tell you his name?"

Danny let one of his arms drop and hung his hand over his knee. "Ah, damn it. Yeah, but I don't remember. It sounded like a Roman name, to be honest. Julius, Gaius, Cassius—" He stopped suddenly as his gaze swept over her. He grimaced. "What happened to you?"

"I've been to varying levels of hell, Danny," she said casually.

"Were you captured?" He moved to jump up as if they were discussing the disgruntled neighbor who'd yelled at her when they were young, and he was about to stomp over there and tell him off like the big brother he was.

She grabbed hold of his shoulders to keep him down. "Stop. I escaped, obviously."

He relaxed slightly, but his face remained twisted in anger. "Why'd they shave your head?"

"They didn't."

"You did that to yourself?" The tightness briefly fell off Danny's face and was replaced with a mildly shocked frown. "I can't say it wasn't a mistake. Sorry."

Catherine rolled her eyes. "Let's just focus on getting Bella back and getting you out of here, please."

"You're not coming with us?"

Catherine looked at him, solemnity and sadness weighing heavily on her. His eyes hinted that the well was far from dry. "I hope to," she said. Giving up was not an option, not when Bowen, Bella, or Danny were involved. She couldn't give up until they were safe. But when the time came? She'd often thought about that quiet peace that giving up would grant.

Lightning flashed, shocking her out of her despair. *Odd,* she thought as it flashed again. The lightning was coming from within the forest, not bleeding down through the trees. Before she could even think about taking cover, several shadow forms appeared one by one, not far from their vulnerable position.

She shot Danny a look. His eyes mirrored her alarm. They stood together as the shadows moved, weaving and bouncing off other shadows until they were only a few feet away. Fae. A bad feeling stormed inside her chest. They looked different from the human-like and frightening childlike fae she'd encountered before. All were draped in gowns of ebony. The white glow from their skin bounced off the black tresses that bobbed around their shoulders.

One of them twisted and contorted, making Catherine jump back, her arms accidentally pushing Danny with her. Moments later, another Danny stood there facing them, only his lopsided smile didn't look so charming on the plotting fae.

Shifters. Bowen had spoken of them once.

Catherine didn't like the look they were giving her—predatory, displaying a raw desire for control. She felt the look crawl over her skin, as though it owned her.

"Leave us alone!" Danny shouted, breaking the trance.

They scowled. "You shouldn't be here. Go," they said in unison. Catherine shivered. "Go now."

"We will, but not without—"

"Go!"

With that, the energy surrounding their bodies moved and bled into them.

Catherine could only watch in horror as the shifters twisted and writhed until they were all the same. They were all Bella. The cheery-eyed woman they both loved stood in a dozen exact replicas.

"Dan? Cathy?" one asked.

Another tilted her head. "What's wrong?"

"No, no, no," Danny mumbled in disbelief.

"None of them is the real her," Catherine warned. "It's just a trick." Though even as she said it, she couldn't help but stare wide-eyed at them.

Danny raised his hands to his head, stretching his elbows back. "I know. She doesn't look like that now."

Catherine turned to her brother. His face was distraught. "What? My God, what happened to her?"

The Bella directly across from Danny stepped forward. "Come with me, Dan," she said in her singsong voice, reaching out for him.

Seeing Danny being pulled in by those big brown eyes, Catherine grabbed his arm. "Don't listen to her!" she yelled. "The real Bella needs you to stay strong." It was enough to make him break eye contact with the shifter.

He directed his gaze to the ground. "I can't do this."

In one swift, inhuman move, one of the copies slid through the space between them. Catherine felt her body hunch into a painful jab to her chest before being knocked backward and falling like a ragdoll to the ground. Bella's laugh rang out, tainted. The sound fell flat on her ears. Her stomach clenched as she struggled beneath the shapeshifter who smiled as she crushed her.

She was losing air and couldn't call out to Danny. She had to get back to him before the shifters separated them. She couldn't see past the black spots.

"Hold me, Dan." The fae locking him in her gaze covered the remaining distance between them and wrapped her arms around him, carefully caressing his unruly hair.

He leaned in and closed his eyes, relaxing into her and holding her tightly. Bella. He had his Bella. Absentmindedly, he ran his fingers through her soft, curly locks.

"Do you like my hair?" she whispered in his ear.

He sighed with pleasure. "Mhmm."

"I can make it however you like. Long, short. Just tell me, and it's done."

Realization shot through his spine, and he stiffened. *Long.* "Long," he mumbled, slowly reopening his eyes.

"Longer than this?"

"Let me show you," he said, and she flinched in confusion. Danny carefully ran his hands through the hair until they were caught in a golden web. "Like this!" He yanked down, snapping the fae's neck in an instant.

Over the shifter's shoulder, he gazed around at the others; there were nine of them ready to pounce. "Bella is Rapunzel," he growled, "and I want Rapunzel!"

"I'm here," they said simultaneously in Bella's cheery voice.

"She isn't here," he said coldly, before shoving the dead copy away from him. Just then he spotted his sister, struggling with another one. "Catherine!"

As he moved toward her, she kicked the shifter with all her

might. He stopped and watched as the fake Bella flew to the ground, fatally hitting her head against some rocks.

When he looked back, four Bellas stood between him and his sister. "Catherine!" Instead of trying to stop him, they twisted and reformed once more. He gasped in horror. Now four exact copies of Catherine stood in front of him.

Five Bellas came up from behind him and twirled him around, and by the time he'd struggled free, it was too late. Five Catherines were scattered on the ground.

"Danny," said one.

"I'm okay," said another.

"Damn it," he muttered, his mind whirling. "Which one?"

Catherine was the first to rise among her doppelgängers. She had an idea. "It's me. Watch," she said, hurrying to her brother's side. "I'm the only one they'll fight."

The others twisted their faces into frowns and scowls. Sensing movement, Catherine glanced at her feet. A white mist was circling their ankles. It rose quickly and then expanded into a thick fog, so thick that she couldn't see her hands when she brought them to her face.

"Catherine!" she heard Danny yell.

She had to call on her magic, however depleted it was. "Hold on," she said, praying she could manipulate her fire into a scorching wind that could blow the fog away. Waving her hands in front of her chest, she outlined an invisible ball. She inhaled, feeling the power rise through her palms. The encased windfire's pressure strained against her hold. She built it up, adding more and more as she focused her mind, tiny sparks flying out from her. Hoping it wouldn't catch Danny in the process, she let go, and it burst out from beneath her hands.

As the wind roared around her, she thought she saw a brief glimpse of him. It blew and beat against everything in its path, growing weaker until it dissipated completely. The fog remained, even thicker than before. How could that be? She had to be able to see to fight. She couldn't stand here helpless. The shapeshifter fae were probably mocking them. She could imagine all five Bellas and all four Catherines wearing smug smiles. She shook her head.

Before Catherine could think of what to do next, a feminine voice sang softly in her ear, and then the sound surrounded her. She couldn't understand the whispered words. "Danny?" she called, hoping he hadn't wandered far. There was no answer.

For the first time since magic began flourishing in her veins, Catherine felt truly freezing. About to bring fire to her palms, she felt a shift in the air, and the song changed with it. The voice grew raspy, more pronounced, escalating from alto to soprano to a horrifying screech. Catherine slapped her cold hands to her ears and dropped to a crouch. She shoved her head between her knees, feeling as though her brain were going to explode.

Suddenly, the incredible voice stopped. Catherine felt relief wash over her. What she wouldn't give to go back to that morning in her warm bed, Bowen's soft breathing the only sound. Was it safe? Slowly she pulled her hands away from her ears. A new fear struck her. Was she deaf? She couldn't even hear her own breathing. She coughed and pulled at her earlobes. Maybe they just needed to pop. Nothing worked. Even in silence, there was some echoing sound, but this was true silence. Nothing.

Acutely aware of how much she relied on her sense of hearing, Catherine felt paranoia set in. She turned every which way, growing more and more frantic. *Oh Bowen, I wish you were here.*

Danny, Bella, I hope you're safe. She was alone. The fae were going to kill her or trap her in this fog forever.

Defeated by her fear, she crumpled to the ground. If it was her entrapment or death they wanted, well, they could have it. She couldn't fight what she couldn't see or hear.

Digging her fingers into the ground, she grabbed hold of damp dirt. Feeling around, her hand grabbed a clump of grass. She moved toward it and curled up on her side, trying to stop shivering. The silence was maddening. Catherine laid her hands over her ears, trying to make herself believe she was just blocking out the normal noises of the world. Then, closing her eyes, she blocked out all thought. She had to focus on her magic. She wouldn't give up just yet. *It's my last hope,* she thought. She felt it grow stronger as her fears subsided, and heat spread through her body. Her hands held most of the magical heat, which provided a comforting sensation as it warmed her ears like earmuffs on a winter's day.

Catherine coughed and reflexively moved to cover her mouth. Had she just heard something crackle? A memory came to mind, that day over a year ago when she and Bowen had stopped their enemy on the battlefield and engaged in a fight to the death. Afterward, her powerful fires had healed her entire wounded body. Besides a random cut or bruise here and there, she hadn't needed to explore that option since then. Until now. Given the struggle to heal her ankle properly, was healing her hearing even possible while being so weak? She had to try. Jumping to action, she sat upright, placed her palms back on her ears, and concentrated. Once more the heat resonated through her, and her body relaxed. How long would it take? Last time, despite the garish wounds all over her body, she had healed instantly without even noticing.

She didn't have time to ponder long. The ground beneath her began to shake violently, and her heart filled with terror. An earthquake? The ground wasn't cracking or rolling yet. She staggered to her feet, and when she managed to catch her balance, the earth stilled. It became visible through the fog then, and she found herself unexpectedly looking at pavement instead of grass and dirt. Looking up, she saw a blue sky appearing. The sound of a large vehicle's exhaust came to her. Was that the sound of a bus? The sound was like heaven. To hear again was bliss. Wait, a bus? Catherine snapped out of her reverie as the sounds around her registered.

All around her the fog was falling away, but Catherine didn't feel like the world was being revealed to her. Instead, she felt she was being revealed to the world. She found herself standing in the middle of Cork.

13

Mary raised her head from the thick-cushioned rocking chair she had fallen asleep in. A feeling that was both cold and hot tingled in her cheeks and in her hands, and she raised her eyebrows in disbelief. The throw blanket fell from her lap as she bolted up. Bursting into Caty and Bowen's room, she gasped. Bowen's body, which had disappeared two days before, had returned.

She grabbed her forehead, trying to work out the worry wrinkles blending with the regular ones, and bent down to touch his hollow-cheeked face. After a few silent seconds she straightened up, her breath flowing easier. He was still alive.

"You don't have much time left in this world, old man," she said, still hovering over him. He didn't flinch, but she hadn't expected him to. Bowen wasn't here. She just hoped he would get back to his body before it was too late.

Resolving to check on it regularly, she left the body in solitude and went outside to her garden. The dusty sunlight on the eastern horizon wasn't strong enough to aid her worn eyes. The corners of her mouth curved upward, and she ran her hands lightly over the flowers as she passed, stopping to smell only a few of her favorites. Giving her senses over to the flowers at least once every day was something she did alone—that is, ever since her husband died many years before. He had been a caring and strong man. The sleeping druid in her home often reminded her of him; he had a similarly kind and old-world spirit. The flowers reminded her of him as well, of working in the garden together, playing in the garden with their children. A lifetime of memories. Flowers were the reason they'd met, and so they'd always brought her joy.

Mary was about to go back inside the house when something in the distance caught her attention. Out among the bushes and the trees stood the hourglass figure of a woman in a green dress. As the light morning fog surrounding the woman began to clear away, Mary could see disheveled red hair billowing around her.

"Is that you, Caty?" Mary's frail voice echoed in the emptiness between them.

The figure didn't move or reply.

"Caty, you must hurry, Bowen's body—"

"Mirn."

Hearing the darkened voice, Mary jerked violently, and she felt the pink vanish from her face. "I didn't think the day would come."

"My release was for their benefit more than mine."

Mary nodded and lightly pursed her lips. *At last,* she thought. "Why have you come to my door?"

"You know why, old friend."

"Aye, I suppose I do," she said with a shaky sigh.

After a few silent moments, the red-haired woman broke the trance. "Go inside, and let me cry for you."

Mary rushed back inside to check on the old man, trying her hardest to ignore the wailing cries outside.

Catherine was blown away. She was in Cork, and at first thought, she had no idea how she'd arrived, though she quickly surmised the fae must be responsible. Why specifically there, at one end of Irish land meeting Irish waters, she couldn't hope to guess. She looked for Danny briefly, but it was clear he wasn't with her. Feeling exposed, she quickly ducked into an empty alley, catching a whiff of the black exhaust spewing out of the bus that had narrowly missed her. Nearby restaurants teased her with the scent of delightful foods carried on the breeze. After checking to make sure nothing was stuck to the bottoms of her feet, she rubbed them rigorously, cursing under her breath. It had been a while since she'd been barefoot on city-paved roads and sidewalks.

Though she hadn't seen a mirror recently, she knew she looked too much of a mess not to draw attention to herself. The unusually bright day was certainly no help. She'd already earned herself a few stares, two obnoxious chuckles, and a few concerned glances. Now somewhat shielded in the alley, she could take a moment to gather her senses.

The last time she'd been to Cork was two years ago with Bella. She grinned, remembering how she'd bored her by dragging her to archaeological sites. Bella would only perk up when they were at restaurants, by the sea, or hiking. The beautiful Currabinny Woods provided a backdrop for a particularly memorable hike. Coinnle corra, more commonly called bluebells, spread out to enjoy the company of trees. Catherine could still hear the excitement in Bella's voice. They'd taken dozens of photos and fallen in the sea of bluebells that rippled like water.

A passerby's stare brought her back to reality with a jolt. She had no money or transportation, and in the human world, she was supposed to be dead. What was she going to do? By car, it would take at least three hours to get back to Mary's house, but without a car she really had no hope.

A few onlookers loitering the connecting sidewalk waved their arms wildly and seemed to be calling for someone else down the street. She carefully peeked out of the alley just as a Garda walked toward them. Quickly sinking back, Catherine cursed and pinched a portion of her skirt, roughly rubbing the fabric between her thumb and middle finger. She looked behind her. The alley was too long. He would see her, even if she ran, but she could get a head start. Her mind spun in panic.

The Garda's footsteps drew nearer, and he stopped in front of them at the end of the alley. Her thoughts were still whirling inside her. "She went down that way," she heard one of them say. "Yeah, she's down there," said another. Her thoughts came to a sudden stop and fixed in place. Instead of running, Catherine boldly stepped out of the alley.

"Miss, are you in a bit of trouble?"

"Yes, I need your help."

"What's your name?"

"I'm Kathleen Green."

The pristine glass throne reflected the lustrous moonlight. On its hard surface rested a withdrawn Judicaël. Though fire had engulfed the throne, it hadn't burned. In fact, it was the only thing left standing in Loïc's castle. At the feet of the high king lay charred rubble that had once been tapestries and finery. He was surrounded by immense chunks of glass, broken tree trunks, and branches. Yet all Judicaël could see were the aural remnants of the woman who dared reject him.

The peculiar glow of her hazel eyes wouldn't leave his thoughts, nor would the curve of her lips, even while disgust that had hung on her every word repeated in his mind, haunting the passing moments since her escape. From his brief contact with her, he felt stronger than he had in centuries. He squeezed his fists together. His knuckles grew another shade of pale, and an old familiar surge ran through him, as powerful as it had been when he last held the energy of a druid's magic so long ago. He had forgotten the alarming difference.

Judicaël knew he was the most powerful and noble in the faerie realm, and that his position of high king was well deserved. Yet he hadn't truly punished the druid woman, hadn't shown her just how strong he was. Though he usually enjoyed the hunt, a small tinge of regret filled him, for if he had, he would still be soaking in her energy and reveling in her presence. The mere memory of her wasn't enough. He wanted her back now. He wanted her to see all of his magnificent strength and for her to fall at his side with desire.

A tapping sound of fingers on glass came from behind him. He didn't bother to look.

"My king." Loïc's voice bounced around the moonlit debris and grated on Judicaël's ears.

"What have you for me, Loïc?" His chest heaved with a deep sigh.

"I've come to offer comfort. This is my castle, and not your glamorous one, lying in shambles at your feet. You need not be so withdrawn."

"Yes, your castle will be rebuilt after the war, Loïc. Never fear."

"I'm not so self-absorbed as that, my king. I still have my throne, protected with my own blood. The end of the war will right all wrongs." When he spoke again, his tone was more deliberate. "Cadeyrn's surrender or death will bring your order back to the kingdoms, and I shall catch this druid woman again. The war and their destruction of my castle shall not go unpunished."

Judicaël shifted in his seat. "Bring her to me."

Loïc's feathered headdress brushed and chimed across his shoulders as he shook his head. "She has a hold on you. Leave her to me—"

"Bring her to me. That is final."

"Yes." Loïc hesitated. "Forgive me."

The high king noticed the quiet scowl as Loïc ran his black and gold eyes over him. "Judicaël," he continued, seemingly taking great effort to control his voice as he walked in a circle around the throne, "rest your noble head, and hush your thoughts." He leaned over his other shoulder from behind the throne's back. "Shall I call the Dullahan to aid in the cause? He will certainly tip the scales of battle in our favor, allowing me the freedom to find her."

"Do as you must," Judicaël replied with a wave of his hand.

"At your will, my king."

At the Garda station in Carrigaline, County Cork, Catherine

sat quietly at a table across from the Garda who'd found her and another who wore an expression of extreme skepticism. She'd just devoured a turkey sandwich and some crisps, and then set to work on a bottle of cold water, fresh from their refrigerator.

"Miss," said the skeptical-looking Garda, "other than the style of your hair, you do match the description of the missing twin. Seems strange you'd come forward now. Were you being held captive all this time?"

"No," she said, memories of being Conall's captive, then the fae's, flashing through her mind. The Gardaí couldn't know an ounce of truth. Not one.

She didn't miss the subtle look that passed between them. She watched them like a hawk. The one who'd brought her in leaned forward and rested his clasped hands on the table. "I know what you told me, but we just want to make sure we cover everything. Now, I won't be asking again. What is your name?"

"My name is Kathleen Green," she repeated. She didn't have time for this. Time in the faerie realm would be moving more quickly, and everyone she loved was counting on her. She needed to get back, and fast. Telling this Garda that she was her deceased sister, who according to their records was only missing, was better than revealing that she, Catherine, had "come back from the dead." It still sparked too many questions for her liking.

"Where have you been, Miss Green?"

"Lost," she said, knowing they wouldn't believe her.

And so, the questioning continued. More looks were exchanged, and then finally, a silent decision to let her rest was made. "Is there anyone you'd like us to contact for you?"

No matter how much she wanted them to contact Mary, she couldn't give them her name. That would lead them too close to everything. She shuddered as she imagined them walking into the cottage and seeing Bowen's unmoving body. "No one."

The other Garda sucked in a breath as he stood and pushed in his chair. "I can see you need some time to process your situation.

I think that's enough questioning for now. How about getting some rest? Is there anything you need? Anything at all?"

"Yes, can you take me somewhere?"

"You want to see someone?"

"Yes, I stayed with some kind strangers who helped me when I needed it most. I promised them I'd retrieve my things I left there. Could someone please drive me?"

He rubbed his chin and glanced at his partner. "I don't see why not." His eyebrows knitted together. "After you've gotten some rest, okay?"

"No!" They looked at her curiously. "I mean, no, please, I'd really like to see them right away so they know I'm all right."

"That's fine," one said with a kind nod.

Catherine sighed inwardly. She liked the Garda, both of them. She wasn't happy about deceiving them, but she didn't have a choice.

They left her at the table and moved toward another desk where they spoke in low tones and went over paperwork. Then the one who'd brought her in left the building, and the other sat down in front of his computer. After waiting ten minutes, Catherine walked over and happened to catch a piece of paper with the name "Daniel Green" next to an old copy of his passport. The Garda quickly shuffled it out of sight. Catherine had forgotten how unhappy Danny always used to look in his official document photos. She had to get back to him.

"I assure you we'll be along soon enough, Miss Green," he said. "Just one more." He clicked away on his computer. "And done." He flashed a winning smile. If he was still skeptical, he was hiding it well.

An hour later, Catherine was sitting in the passenger seat of the Garda's car, dressed in a second-hand pair of blue jeans, a women's T-shirt, and a light windbreaker with a hood. She was grateful for the clothing, especially the hooded jacket. So far it seemed no one had noticed the patterns sticking out from under the tattered scarf. Regardless, she was happy to hide in the hood.

"I hope they fit well. My young one's up in Dublin for college and left some things behind."

College. It seemed like a lifetime ago. Three years had passed faster than she could have believed. "Yes, thank you, and thank her for me."

"Oh, not a problem. Glad to help any way I can. I thought you looked about the same size."

They sat in silence as the compact car marked with "Garda" on the side carried them across the motorway. As the beautiful Irish landscape rolled by, tree-speckled green hills rising between large empty grasslands, all Catherine could think about was Danny. What had happened to him? Was he okay? The shapeshifters had been alarmed by their presence, that's why they were intimidating them. Otherwise, they would have just killed them. Or maybe they wanted to capture them, make them prisoners of war. Her breath caught in her throat. She had to find out if Danny had escaped.

Another hour and forty minutes passed, and then they were in Dublin. The nostalgia hit her instantly, and she was able to forget her predicament for a moment to revel in the return to her old home. The city where she'd started her career, the city where she'd met Bowen and Bella. The Spire stood solid and true. She gazed out the window at the colorful old-style buildings. She missed walking among them. Pedestrians crowded every bridge over the River Liffey, which reflected the gray sky hanging over its waters.

"Where will it be then?" the Garda asked, startling her. She'd forgotten he was even there. "Do they live in the city center?"

"I hate to trouble you so much, you've been so kind to me already, but do you mind if I call my friends before I drop in? I should have thought about it before we left." She squinted and sunk in on herself as the lie fell from her mouth.

"Sure, sure, Miss Green. Not a problem."

With some skilled maneuvering, he pulled up to one of the many internet cafés. "Here you go," he said, handing her a twenty euro note. She felt another pang of guilt. "I'll wait here."

She thanked him and went inside. A man at the front desk led her past the aisles of the many in-use computer stations and down the phone booth aisle to an open compartment. As soon as she closed the door behind her, she dialed Mary's number. Where would she even start? The phone rang and rang. Mary didn't pick up. Catherine had been counting on Mary's being there for Bowen. Maybe something had happened. No, it was probably a simple explanation. She could very well be out on one of her walks or working in the gardens.

Catherine hung up the phone. She'd planned on giving the remaining money back, but without Mary's help, she needed it. Hurriedly, she moved back to the front of the shop and peered cautiously out. The Garda was still in his car, looking in the other direction. Holding her breath, she slipped out and speed-walked to keep up with passersby and use them as cover until she was well out of his range of view.

She made it to the rails in no time and left on the next train. As it pulled out of the station, Catherine felt a mix of relief and guilt flood through her. She was free from skeptical eyes, but the Garda had been kind. Gazing out at Dublin as it passed by her window, she relaxed into her seat. She hated taking advantage of people but considering the lives depending on her, it couldn't be helped. Catherine wrapped her arms around her middle, and on one side she rubbed a piece of her second-hand jacket's fabric between her fingertips. At least the Garda would get to pay an unexpected visit to his daughter now because of her.

14

AFTER GETTING OFF THE TRAIN, Catherine ran into the minister who'd performed her marriage. Driving along in his car, Pastor Kelley had almost passed her before he recognized who she was as she hurried down the side of the rural road. She sighed in great relief when he agreed to take her the rest of the way home. She was so close now.

She burst into the cottage. Finding no one in the living area, she rushed to her bedroom to find Bowen's body, still as a statue. Before she could process what she was seeing, she heard movement behind her, and she whirled around. To her utter shock, a shapeshifter with jet black hair and clothing stood in the doorway.

Catherine instantly filled her palms with fire.

"Caty, stop, it's me!"

She froze. That voice. Her eyes widened and she quickly drew back her power, straightening up. "Mary?" She blinked a few times. It couldn't be.

"That's right, Caty," she cooed, her voice now young and steady, an otherworldly echo behind it. "I'm one of the wee-folk."

Catherine's gaze narrowed. "How do I know you're not just a shifter pretending to sound like Mary?"

"Would any other shifter know that your uncle was the first person who sensed magic hidden inside you?"

She'd never told anyone but Bowen and Mary about the hushed conversation she'd shared with her late uncle years before. It was her.

"But how?" How had she never seen it? Even a hint? Had Bowen?

"I was born fae. I lived in my realm for centuries, but I fell in love with the human realm the minute I first stepped into it, so I stayed."

Catherine sat down on the bottom corner of the bed and rested her hands on her knees for support as she took in this unbelievable thing she couldn't wrap her head around. "But what about your family? Did they know?"

Mary's long-legged fae body, so vastly different from her human form, moved through the room to the windowsill. She gracefully leaned against it. "Aye, my Connor knew. Out of all the flowers he could have, he plucked me." She smiled, seeming to reminisce.

Catherine watched her carefully, still unnerved. Fascination ended up adding to the mix of feelings rushing around inside her.

"I met my Connor that first day in the human realm, and he was the most beautiful thing I'd ever seen. I've seen other worlds of unimaginable beauty, but not one of them could hold up next to him in my eyes."

Catherine knew exactly how Mary felt. It was the same for her with Bowen. It was as though he had been made just for her and she for him. When she looked at him, all she saw was happiness. Nothing could ever match the beauty he radiated.

Mary chuckled lightly. "He told me he had never taken the time to look at flowers, never cared for them, but that day was fated. He was always trying to get away from the fighting inside his house. He usually didn't have to go far, but that day it was far too boorish and loud, so he left, not worried about ever going back. That day, he decided to walk in the gardens his mother had planted, far out past the ruins." She sighed happily. "I had just stepped out, and was enjoying the difference in the air you breathe here, and the way things look and feel. I was soaking everything in when I heard him coming. Instead of leaving, I changed myself into a flower. He walked around for a time, and I watched him intently. I still remember my heart speeding up as he strolled straight up to me as if he could tell I was different."

Catherine was warmed by the image.

"Then he plucked me, inhaled my fragrant scent, and when he drew back, I changed back into the form you see now."

"Was he scared of you?" Catherine asked despite herself.

Mary's lips curled into another knowing smile. "No, and I was surprised he wasn't. Love can happen when you first meet, and it did for us. I never left his side. We married, had a family. When he and our offspring passed away, I was left with our life here, and this immortality became a curse. Now you know why I could often relate to the tortures Bowen faced for so long."

Catherine couldn't imagine such a thing. What Bowen had gone through was terrible enough, but being sentenced to immortality alone after knowing one true love? That wound could never heal. Bowen had narrowly missed the same fate as Mary when Catherine nearly recast the curse on Conall the year before. She hoped that her time living under the same roof as Mary had helped ease the woman's suffering, even a little.

The eddying thoughts in Catherine's mind took another turn down Curiosity Lane. "I've never seen a photo of you when you were young," she said carefully, her hands fidgeting a little. "Did you manage to look human then too?"

Mary stretched her arms above her head. "Aye," she said. "I'm a shifter, so I can look more human and age myself. It feels good to change back all the way sometimes, though." She dropped her arms back down.

Catherine let the words sink in a moment. "If your children died, well . . . is Kenneth actually your grandson?"

"That he is. I took him in when he was young, after his father died. My son wasn't a child when he passed, but too young to go." She moved her gaze to the ground, trying to find something to focus on.

"Does Kenneth know?"

Mary nodded. "When he found he had no magic of his own, he grew unmanageable and quickly started obsessing about it. He has always hungered for power, almost more than a full-blooded fae." She jerked her head up and looked directly at Catherine. "Listen to me, Caty. The banshee's wailing song sings the name of Mirn. I don't have much time."

A banshee? Yet another Irish legend was real? Perhaps it was morbid, but Catherine had always found the myth of the banshee fascinating. A female spirit whose wailing warns of impending death on a household or individual within. She suddenly straightened. Could that be the origin of the screams on the wind she'd heard before? Catherine furrowed her brow, trying to imagine the fae creature of legend. *Wait, who?* "Who is Mirn?"

Mary's hands shook slightly before she clasped them together. "I'm Mirn, and I already suspect how it will end for me. I don't want to die at the hand of my grandson."

Catherine's eyebrows shot up. "What are you talking about?"

"He'll come back here the first chance he can." Mary sighed. "I've known this, and since things didn't go his way before, I don't think he's willing to wait any longer."

She couldn't stand this. "I don't understand. Why would Kenneth try to kill you?"

"Because he thinks my magic will go into him if he takes my life. He read some of my books and mistranslated one. He's only ever seen me as an elderly woman, not visibly a fae, so he held off when he learned of other ways he could gain power. A power even stronger than mine. I've always known he would be back for me when he failed at all the others. The banshee's call means the time is now."

"But Mary—I mean, are you sure?"

"I'm sure of it, and my magic is only as good as my shifting form." She paused. "Meaning I can't shift into someone or something more powerful than myself in order to stop him, and I can't use my magic to fight anymore. I sacrificed those abilities trying to heal my family a long time ago."

Catherine couldn't imagine what Mary's long life must have been like in the fae realm. Given everything that changed for her own life once curses, druids, and magic came into it, she was curious but mostly saddened for Mary's obviously tragic attempt at leading a human lifestyle. "Then just tell him that," she said, wanting to scream in frustration. "If he turns up here one day. Maybe he won't try to kill you then. Why are you worried when there's nothing left there for him to take?"

Mary shook her head. "Because deep within me still lurks dangerous energy, which someone else can use. I don't want it to go to waste if he is the one to kill me, and I will die soon, somehow. The banshee doesn't make a mistake."

"You don't have to accept this fate. We should fight together! As a shifter, you can hide and trick him, do anything to stop him."

"You know as well as I do what needs to be done."

"What? If not fight, then what?"

"The book he mistranslated explains that my magic can go into the person who kills me, but only if I give it over," Mary said, her voice flat. "If you take my magic, you will get enough strength to live a little longer. Long enough to save Bowen." Catherine needed that chance to save Bowen more than anything, but not at such a cost. She couldn't. She started to protest, but Mary raised a firm hand. "It must be done."

This couldn't be the only way. She could feel the tears welling in her eyes. "I can't do this, Mary, I just can't! Please don't make me do this. Please!"

Mary just looked at her with a small smile. "It must be done in blood, not magic." Hidden within her black garments, she withdrew a beautifully ornate dagger Catherine had never seen before. Its style wasn't something recognized as being from any modern human culture, in fact, it resembled some of the ancient jeweled daggers she saw within Gwenaël's mirror. Mary reached out and took her hands and wrapped them around the hilt. "Make it swift and final, or I'll suffer."

"No! This is wrong!" Catherine sobbed, and her voice broke. "There has to be another way."

"I'd rather die with you than with my grandson, Caty. I've been alive for centuries. This isn't a tragedy. My time has come." Catherine raised her eyes and met Mary's gaze. "I'll be going to meet my family again, Caty. Don't be saddened by this." But how could she not be? Through love, Mary was part of her family as well. She didn't want to lose her.

"Mary," she said, and the fae shapeshifter with the soul of Mary tilted her head with a smile. "Please," Catherine whispered.

"No, dear. My energy must pass on to the next stage. Take my magic, and use it to help keep the human realm safe."

Keep the human realm safe. The words repeated over and over in Catherine's mind, an internal chant slowly building her courage.

Mary looked at Bowen then back to her. "Not here. The old man doesn't need any more death around him." She swept out of the room. Reluctantly, Catherine followed, gripping the weapon.

When they reached the middle of the living area, Mary stopped in front of the couch. Catherine was suddenly aware that Mary now towered over her. "Once I'm gone, my energy will pass on to you almost immediately. Wait for it, and you'll see," she said with a sad smile as she softly caressed her cheek. "It's time now." She dropped her hand. "Strike."

Catherine took one long look at the being she'd grown to love as another mother, heard the blood pounding in her ears. She breathed in so sharply the air sliced at her expanding insides. With a determined movement, she thrust the dagger into Mary's chest as hard as she could. The slick sound but rough jerk of it made Catherine sick to her core. She felt the blood leave her face. Mary cringed a moment, and then, as she relaxed into the dagger, she whispered, "Thank you, Caty."

"I'll miss you, Mary," she whispered back.

Mary slumped down into the couch. Dark pools of blood soaked her clothes and seeped into the couch cushions. She closed her eyes, let out a long sigh, and didn't breathe in again.

Catherine stood over her body, shaking from the inside out. *What have I done?* As her trembling hands slowly pulled the dagger free, she felt a cold sensation before something warm bloomed and spread through her fingers and into her body, strengthening as it went. The poised and lovely Mary, the shapeshifter Mirn, was now a part of her.

Even though she'd rigorously scrubbed her hands, Catherine still didn't feel clean. She moved on to her arms. All she could hear was Mary's voice in her head: *Caty, Caty, Caty.* She was just thankful Mary had remained in her fae form. *Of course,* Catherine thought. *She shifted for that very reason.* Releasing a shaky breath, she dried her hands and arms on a towel, then on her jeans, and left the bathroom, avoiding eye contact with the mirror.

She returned to Bowen. His pallid face and closed eyes felt like a wall between them. *Oh Bowen,* she thought, moving toward the bed. *I would give anything to talk to you. Open your eyes, smile at me.* She kissed his hand then his lips, wishing she were in a fairy tale and this was enough to wake him.

She heard Mary's voice in her mind again. *Keep the human realm safe*. She needed some air.

In Mary's gardens that skirted the old cottage, Catherine fiddled with the cleaned dagger as she sat on a cold stone slab and gazed up the path leading to the open land where the ruins stood. Beyond that, the faerie realm waited for her. She needed a plan. Running back into the forest without clear knowledge of where Danny and Bella were would result in getting lost or captured again. Plus, what was she going to do once she found them? Run back home and have the fae follow her? No, she had to figure out a way to prevent the fae from ever getting to her again. Otherwise, all of this was for nothing. Even if Cadeyrn could stop the war, based on what she'd seen in Judicaël's personality, she wasn't so sure her rejection of him or destroying a fae castle changed or quieted his desire for her.

I'll tear down your realm.

Catherine inhaled sharply at the memory. Yes, she had to cut off the fae realm, trap them somewhere else. Plucking them like unruly weeds and leaving them alone together was the only solution.

Suddenly the face of a beautiful woman framed with flowing red hair appeared closely in front of her. Too startled to react fully, Catherine felt a scream lodge itself in the back of her throat.

"You have Mirn's energy." The fluid voice seemed to float in the air around them.

Catherine nodded stiffly.

"Mirn is gone," the woman said sorrowfully, sinking backward.

She knows Mary's faerie name. Catherine found her voice. "Fae?"

The woman shrugged and stood up. Her waist-length hair spilled out around her. "I knew the shapeshifter well. A long time ago."

"I'm sorry," Catherine said under her breath.

"She is safely sleeping now. A far better fate than mine."

"Why do you say that?"

"My existence has been used for nothing but weeping over what was lost and what is yet to be lost. My wails are the warning."

Catherine silenced a gasp. "You're the banshee."

"I am the last."

Catherine's imagination went wild. What could have happened to leave only one? How many were there to begin with? Until this faerie civil war, she had thought every fae was immortal. Apparently, this eerie female creature was as sorrowful inside as she appeared out. At least she wasn't out to kill her. At that thought, Catherine felt the hot bubbles of sweat on her body momentarily cool.

Catherine suddenly realized she was staring and hadn't said anything for a while. She cleared her throat. "The last?" She couldn't help but gape at the human-like beauty of this fae. Somehow the sadness in her eyes, her tearful-sounding voice, the tragedy of her very being, all of it created a strange kind of beauty that melded with her alluring features.

The banshee ran her slender fingers through her disheveled red tresses and solemnly gazed away from Catherine. "A long story I shall not reveal to you." She was clearly affronted. "Humans are far too prideful. They pry into everything. I'd forgotten."

Catherine felt her cheeks grow hot. The banshee was right, but the fae's sudden mood swing alarmed her. *Does she know my lock of hair was the catalyst that set the war in motion? Were the other banshees killed in it, or before?* So many lingering questions she didn't dare ask.

The banshee continued. "The human descendants I've let down, I've let down for far too long. They are no longer in need of me." She spoke the last words so low that Catherine barely caught them. "But I tried. I tried! I was caged for too many years."

She couldn't stop the question from escaping. "Who released you?"

"I do not know my rescuer, but given his deceptive visage, I suspect the act worked in his favor." She shook her head. "I care not about his plans. I'll do as I will and finish my role in this world." Swiping her hand through the air as she turned back, forlorn and troubled. "There isn't time. Many lifetimes will have passed telling these tales. You must go. The war waits for you. I will stay and weep for your coming death."

"Wait a minute, you can see that for sure?" She knew it was coming, but she didn't think she'd be given official notice.

"You do not strike me as being arrogant." The banshee kept an unblinking, steady gaze as she spoke. "You are very strong, but the fae you go up against are stronger still. It is likely you will not survive." Catherine remained silent, unsure how she should feel with too many feelings to count. The fae woman continued. "Heed my warning: the footsteps of a fae will lead you to your death, or a death trap that very few can save you from."

Catherine thought briefly of the Irish and other faerie tales she'd read as a child. They'd always made her think of the fae as both beautiful and wonderful. In her dreams, their magic was used purely for good, as a way to help her make sense of all the evil in the world. There was a time when she'd thought faerie footprints were specks of magic left behind that the earth couldn't bear parting with.

The banshee drew close, interrupting her thoughts. Without a word, she lifted Catherine's forearm, and after a moment's pause midair, placed a golden feather into her palm. Loïc's? It was just like the ones from his headdress. Catherine looked up at the fae's mysterious face. "What is this for?"

"An advantage," she said flatly.

Catherine looked at it more closely, and seeing nothing unusual about it, wondered just what advantage one of Loïc's feathers could give her. "I don't understand," she said, meeting the fae's eyes.

"Loïc uses blood magic in all that he owns, even his throne, to keep them from being destroyed. When separated, the feather will sense he is near. That knowledge will protect you." She stepped away from her, letting go of her forearm.

"Thank you." Catherine smiled.

"I do this for Mirn," the woman said as she turned and walked away.

"Wait. How can I find you to return it?"

"You won't. However, after the winds hear your name cry from my lips, I can find you anywhere." A shiver moved down Catherine's back. She didn't like that a banshee was going to keep tabs on her. "Go," the beautiful banshee said, interrupting her thoughts. "I must weep."

Fearing how strong the sound of the banshee's wail would be this close, Catherine quickly hid the feather in her pocket, then carefully slipped the dagger between her lower back and the waist of her jeans. She covered her ears with both hands as she fled. She couldn't allow her ears to bleed, she needed every sense and ability at her disposal. After putting some space between her and the banshee, she let her hands drop. She'd walked a few paces when the loud wailing on the wind became the horrid screech she'd heard before entering the black forest. Then a chilling thought struck her. *Who was she crying for then?*

15

Catherine didn't feel at all settled by the knowledge that she was going to die. By all accounts, she figured she should have been dead already, but still, to have heard it from the caller of death herself—now it was written in ink.

It doesn't matter, she reminded herself. Just as long as she didn't die before she finished her task. The black forest loomed high above her once again. Only this time, the energy was less frightening and more worrisome. Catherine shivered as a tingling sensation migrated up her arms that resulted in a black hole in her stomach. Her chest felt as though it were about to shatter. One more loss was all it would take. Kathleen and Mary were gone forever. Bowen, Danny, and Bella were next. She silently repeated their names and then instantly regretted it. What if the banshee caught her words on the wind?

She plunged into the blackness, but this time she wasn't lost. Thanks to the banshee's gift, she guessed she could use it to find out the way she had taken before and then avoid it completely. She stopped long enough to take out the golden feather, and with no noticeable change, she gripped it tightly as she sprung forward.

Only a short time passed before a light started flashing in her eyes from below. Catherine stopped and looked at the golden feather. It was glowing. It wasn't very bright, only a glimmer, but it might as well have been a spotlight in the black forest. She walked for a time and realized that traveling in one direction caused the feather's light to grow in intensity, and when she backed up it lessened dramatically. *"Loïc uses blood magic in all that he owns,"* the banshee had said, *"even his throne."* Satisfied, she hid it back in her pocket, and once her eyes adjusted to the darkness once more, she ran up a different path. She knew the definite direction to avoid now, the one that would've taken her straight back to Loïc's broken castle. His throne must have still been intact, or if not, she didn't want to meet him alone on the road. The question she kept asking herself now was, is this path a safer one? Would it lead her to her brother and Bella somehow? Cadeyrn had said he was going to the battle in the north. Maybe she could find him again and this time ask for help.

Catherine pulled at all her magical senses to avoid stumbling or jumping in fear every time a noise approached. Thankfully no shapeshifters, lower or higher kings, vindictive queens, or any other fae were in sight. The war hadn't reached this far except in a political sense. She supposed this made things more dangerous for her personally, as the origin of the lock.

She made it out of the black forest and into another set of faerie woods. Thin beams of light streamed down between the trees. Though she was running like she'd never run before, the strange space and time of the fae realm made her efforts feel futile. Distracted, her senses followed suit, and suddenly, she bumped into something and her feet flew out from underneath her. Gritting her teeth, she jumped back up, ready to fight. Looking back at her were two large brown eyes filled with terror.

"Bella!" She reached for her friend and wrapped her in a crazed hug, too shocked to cry. *It's really her,* she repeated over and over, needing to convince herself. *It's really her.* "Are you all right?"

"Sweet Cathy," Bella said, sobbing into her shoulder. "You came to save me too?"

"Of course I did!" Catherine said, releasing her friend so she could look at her. "No one can keep me away."

Bella jumped forward into another hug.

"Danny told me what happened," Catherine mumbled into Bella's hair. "I didn't think I'd find you before someone got you again." She pushed some hair out of the way, but more gathered in front of her mouth.

Bella pulled out of the hug, and Catherine got a real look at her this time. *Poor Bella. You've been to hell and back.* Her face was dirty and tear-stained, and the golden curls that usually framed her face hung limply, dull and murky from days of dirt and sweat. Was it her imagination, or was it longer too?

"It's revolting, Cathy."

"What is?"

"Look." Bella shifted her body slightly, and Catherine felt her eyes grow and grow as she took in the excessively long locks flowing across the forest behind her friend. She met Bella's gaze and cleared her throat. Was this the spell Danny had been talking about?

"I hate it. It's heavy and hot, and I just want it to go away."

Catherine pulled out her dagger. "Maybe I can chop it off." After facing Bella away from her and having her rest on her knees, Catherine carefully weaved the hair out of her way and leaned down. She placed some of the hair over the widest rock she could find, lodged in the ground nearby, and began sawing away. If she could just saw that off, Bella's hair would only come down to her knees.

Bella sighed with relief. "Oh, thank you."

Catherine could feel sweat quickly building on her brow, not from the effort but from the worry. It didn't matter if she used deliberate or quick motions, the hair would not be cut. Each strand refused and resisted the dagger's sharp blade. She let the blade clatter against the rock. "I can't, it won't. It's not working." Catherine slumped and sat back on her feet. They were silent for a moment. The area reeked of disappointment.

"It's okay," Bella said, breaking the silence. "With your brother's help, I managed. We can do it too." Her lips quivered slightly as she tried to smile, and the very sight threatened to drop Catherine's heart to the pit of her stomach.

"Actually, he should be back soon. He just went to check ahead." Bella sighed as she looked over her shoulder into the forest. "Hopefully he won't get lost, he did drop the 'rope.'" She shook a piece of her hair for emphasis.

Catherine blinked in momentary confusion. "Danny just now left you? So he's all right! I was so scared those shifters killed him."

Bella snapped around, brows furrowed. "What? Shifters?"

"He didn't tell you what happened to us?" Why wouldn't he tell her?

"Cathy, what are you talking about? Dan never mentioned anything like that. He came in here to find me, and we've been running ever since."

"But—" Catherine pursed her lips for a second before suddenly reeling back. "I must have come back here at the same time I was taken out," she babbled.

"Cathy?"

She looked back at the puzzled and concerned Bella. "Sorry, it's complicated." Standing, she adjusted her plan. "Listen, we have to go. Danny might still be in danger." Just remembering the shifters' attack made Catherine clench her fists.

Bella looked worried. "I'll only slow you down, but I know it's out of the question that you'll leave me to go save him."

"You're right. I won't. Danny wouldn't want that either." She put the dagger back in her jeans before grappling with her friend's hair. "I'm getting you both out of here, or I'll die trying."

"How can we possibly get to him like this?" Bella sighed.

"We can do this." Carefully, she handed a large armful to Bella and smirked. "At least you're not bald."

Bella frowned. "Please, I'd rather be bald than get to say I know how Rapunzel must have felt." She drew back in surprise when Catherine removed her hood and the worn scarf she'd left on as an extra precaution.

"I'm so sorry, all that lovely hair."

Catherine couldn't restrain a chuckle. "It seems to be my destiny to suffer in every way possible," she said with a shrug. "Look, my hair doesn't matter. We've got to get you out of here first. I think I know the way I came in this time. I'll come back for Danny, he'd wouldn't want you anywhere near those shifters."

"I can't—"

"I'll help you with the Rapunzel hair. Come on," she said, picking up more coils.

"No, Cathy, I can't," she said, grabbing her arms.

Catherine bent down to where Bella still sat. What was she talking about? "Why?"

"I can't move my legs. Before you bumped into me I was barely conscious. I just kept thinking that Dan would come back any minute," she grabbed her stomach as if something had made her queasy, "and the next thing I knew you were there to save me."

"I don't think I can carry you out of here, Bella."

Bella dropped her chin to her chest. "Bricius cursed me. If I left his cage, I'd fall asleep."

"That doesn't sound so bad."

"Forever, Cathy." She closed her eyes. "Forever."

Catherine slapped her face. "Stop that!" Much to her relief, Bella opened her eyes again almost instantly. "If that's true, how did you keep running with my brother?"

Bella snickered, almost snorting. "It's not funny, it just sounds . . ." She began dozing again.

Catherine brought her back with another swift slap.

"What, Bella?"

"He kissed me."

True love's kiss, she thought. *Of course.* Danny had no magic of his own, and the only knowledge he had of anything related to legends and mythology was through retellings of fairy tales. She'd always known he secretly loved Bella, and she'd suspected Bella felt the same about him. Since the kiss worked, she obviously did, but the spell was apparently too powerful to break that way.

Bella slumped forward, startling Catherine. She grabbed her friend by both shoulders and shook her until her head bobbed back up. "You've got to stay awake, Bella! Do you hear me?"

"Yes," she mumbled. "Yes, find him."

Who knows where he could be? I might be too late already, she thought, her frustration growing. There was no time to lose. Without hesitation, she put her hands on either side of Bella's face and planted a kiss on her lips. Bella jolted back suddenly, as if she'd been holding her breath and could now exhale again.

Catherine smiled. "It worked!"

"Cathy, you didn't have to do that." Bella covered her mouth, and the flush across her cheeks showed through all the dirt smudges.

"Yes, I did. A kiss is a kiss, and I'll do it again as long as it saves you," she declared. She set her jaw as she helped Bella stand.

"There you are, my beauty," said a slithery voice from behind her. Catherine jumped out of her skin. "Ugh, this language."

She whirled around. Out from behind one of the trees walked a fae. His deliberate, slow footsteps made no crunching sound on the forest floor, as though he were walking on air.

"Is this the one?" she whispered, looking over her shoulder at Bella, who only nodded in reply.

The fae grinned. "I think she's rather shy around me."

"That's enough, don't come any closer."

"Bricius."

Catherine frowned. "What?"

"That's my name."

"Right. I could really care less."

Bricius shrugged. "You're much nicer than the last one."

"I mean it, stop where you are!"

He stopped, but reluctance painted his face. "Fine, I'll play your game."

Catherine narrowed her eyes. "I'm not playing any games. Leave Bella and me alone. You don't know who you're dealing with."

"What makes you say that? I know everything there is to know about you. Honestly, so do a few other fae."

She eyed him a moment before scoffing. "You know nothing."

Bricius chuckled and folded his long arms across his chest.

"Fine. What, then?"

He didn't seem in any hurry to answer. Catherine felt sick as fascination filled his eyes. One hand fiddled with the long black braid hanging over his shoulder. Everything about him made Catherine want to vomit, and based on Bella's expression, she was definitely thinking the same thing.

"I don't think we have time to go into that." He gestured to Bella. "Tell me, how are you still awake, my lovely?"

Bella cringed.

Catherine stepped in front, shielding her from the disgusting fae. "Not. Your. Lovely," she growled.

"Well," he said, letting out an annoyed huff as he calmly folded his arms. "In case you're wondering, the only one who can break the spell is me. You're truly wasting your time. Just come back with me, and you won't have to worry about it anymore."

No, she'll just become your personal statue until her body can no longer be magically sustained, and then she'll die. Catherine wanted to say this aloud but gritted her teeth instead. *Dammit.* There had to be another way to break the spell. Returning Bella to the human realm might do it, but that was only a theory. She had very little time left to find an answer.

"Cathy, please."

Bella needed another kiss. Then another thought occurred to her. Catherine moved to grab hold of her friend but turned at the last minute, just as Bricius approached, and gave him the kiss instead. If giving Bella a kiss of true love was enough to confuse the spell, then maybe sacrificing herself out of love for Bella could break it. Bricius violently pushed her away, but it was too late. Almost instantly, the shine returned to Bella's hair, and Catherine felt her scalp begin to itch and burn. The discomfort overwhelmed her, and she screeched, tearing at her head.

The sensation didn't last long. Catherine managed to stand straight with Bella's help, but before she could thank her, she was overcome with another strange sensation.

"Your hair!" Bella shouted.

Catherine gasped at the sight of tens of thousands of wavy red strands growing down past her face. When they reached to just above her collarbone, she no longer felt the odd sensation. Catherine moved her hands along the sides of her face and felt her pulse skip a few beats when the ridges of her fingers found nothing but flawless skin. The lines were gone. She grabbed hold of her hair and reveled in the feeling of being one step closer to her old self.

Bricius scowled. "How did you know that would break my spell?"

"I know power you can never have."

"I was wrong," he said with a sneer. "You're far crueler than the other one. It doesn't matter that you won this battle, because I'll win the war when Loïc drains the rest of your oathing stone."

Catherine struggled to keep her face calm as her stomach clenched. "How did he get it?" From the moment she'd met Loïc, she'd known he had something to do with it. How could Loïc have known what her oathing stone was in the first place? Again she thought of Bowen, limp and helpless at home. Picking an oathing stone that connected them to their ancestors and the land had been like putting a giant red dot on their backs for every Irish fae to spot.

From the corners of her eyes, she could see falling waves of red. Her hair was continuing to grow back. A sudden realization hit her. *I must have broken the protection spell.* Had she just marked her own time of death with a kiss? Again, she fought to keep her face from giving her thoughts away.

"I told you, I know everything about you. Cadeyrn gave it to him. You should have thrown it into the sea instead of placing it by that useless old oak. I couldn't have stolen it from the water."

She closed her eyes, trying to get the words to sink in, struggling to process one tide of knowledge at a time. Cadeyrn had lied to her? He was the one fae besides Mary and the banshee that she'd trusted. She cursed herself for fixating on his one act of kindness. Of course he'd lied. Cadeyrn was Bricius' king, and she had been a pawn. Bricius had probably been watching her for God knows how long, and he'd stolen the oathing stone at his king's bidding to give to Loïc. *But why? Maybe my lock and stone, along with the ancient power of a druid's vow of eternal love, will strengthen their kingdom so they can overthrow Judicaël.*

She shook her head. She couldn't focus on the why right now. "That stone is mine, and I'm taking it back," she said, glaring more with each syllable she uttered.

"If Cadeyrn doesn't finish you with your infamous lock first," he said snidely.

Bella balled her fists and planted her feet. "Go away, you disgusting sliver of a thing!"

Amusement danced in Bricius' eyes. "Why should I? I can just recast the spell."

"Not if I burn you to a crisp right now," Catherine added.

He flinched for a second, but his calm gaze soon returned, followed by a knowing smile. "If you do, then how will you ever have the strength to fight everyone else who's after you?"

It happened in an instant. The fire enclosed his feet in a circle, and as he screamed, the flames shot fiercely upward, encasing him. It quickly simmered. There were no more screams. Only ashes.

"Like that," Catherine said to the ashes, and silently thanked Mary's energy. Turning to Bella, whose jaw looked tight and eyes gaping, she grasped her hand tightly. "Now he can't ever hurt you again," she whispered.

Bella still looked shaken, but relieved.

"Come on." Catherine gestured with her head toward the path that had led her to Bella. "It's this way."

"I loved your beautiful wedding, but I think if I ever get out of here, I'm not coming back for a visit," Bella said dryly.

Catherine let out a small humorless laugh. Her wedding day had been beautiful, but that's all it had been. A day. She and Bowen had been cheated of their future. The wedding seemed so long ago now, and the distance between her and her love was so far and so thick with fog that she couldn't imagine it ever clearing.

They moved down the path slowly at first then picked up the pace for a time, but soon Bella stopped.

"What's wrong?"

Bella sighed. "I'm just tired because I haven't eaten or slept in so long."

Catherine had forgotten about that. The faerie realm's time really did do strange things to the human body. How else could they still be functioning as well as they were? "Come here," she said, wrapping her arms around her friend. "It's okay." Within seconds, Bella's head fell on her shoulder, and she was out.

Great, Catherine thought. *Standing alone in a fae forest with sleeping Rapunzel on my shoulder is just what I need right now.* She was vulnerable. Fae could be lurking everywhere, and she and Bella were in the middle of an open path. Before she could start dragging Bella in hopes of resting against a tree, something rustled behind her.

"Could always drop her. With that much hair, she probably wouldn't even notice."

Catherine shuddered. She recognized the snarling tone.

"Though if it were me, I'd just throw the pile of fleas."

Kenneth. She snapped her head around. He stood holding a handful of Bella's hair, a scowl on his tanned face. Mary's grandson. "How did you get away from the Gardaí?"

The last time she'd seen Kenneth was at her old museum when he'd tricked her and Bowen to get them there. They had to knock him out to escape the trap he'd set, leaving him to take the fall for stealing their much-needed magical relic.

He clicked his tongue. "Cathy, Cathy, Cathy," he said, shaking his head. Catherine felt her skin crawl. "I was never caught."

"What?" She knew she looked as unbelieving as she felt. "Then why didn't you—"

"Come after you? I knew I couldn't get to you in time for the relic again, and I knew Gran didn't want me back, so I stayed in Dublin. I've been biding my time, watching and waiting."

Catherine flinched in confusion. "What are you talking about? Watching and waiting for what?"

Bella whimpered and lifted her head off her shoulder. "Cathy?" she whispered.

"Are you all right now?"

Bella grabbed her head and winced. "I think so." Kenneth tugged harshly on the clump of hair he still gripped, and she quickly turned. At the sight of his smug face, she let out a yelp. "Ken!" she yelled in disgust.

He shifted his features briefly to a smirk before he switched to solemnity, and spoke with mock concern. "Hi, my dear. Why haven't you answered my calls?"

"My God. How'd you find me?"

"Kenneth is your ex?" No, it couldn't be true.

"Much to my dismay. You know him?"

Just then the figure of a disheveled man appeared from the

other side of the overgrown path they stood in. "Bella!" he shouted. Bella gripped Catherine's hands tighter, but the latter gave a small sigh of relief as recognition dawned. Danny.

He rushed over. "You're both here!" He gathered each of them into a tight hug. "God, I didn't think I'd ever see either of you again!"

"Did the shapeshifters hurt you?" Catherine asked, keeping a watchful eye on Kenneth.

He pulled back and shrugged. "Not much," he said with a grin. "No really, they knocked me out in that fog, and when I woke up, I was alone."

Bella sighed. "I'm so glad you're okay, Dan."

With a longing gaze, he moved the loose strands in her face away from her eyes.

"Me too," said Catherine, grabbing his shoulder and breaking him out of his trance. No time for that.

He met her gaze. "It's nice to see you with hair again." He winked and then tipped away in a hurry when she pinched his shoulder.

"I'm really tired of getting interrupted," Kenneth grumbled. "I don't have time for this."

Danny turned to the voice and furrowed his brow. "Hey, I know you."

Catherine looked at her brother curiously. "I thought you never met Bella's ex?"

"What?" He raised his eyebrows. "I haven't. This is the guy who came to the house to see Kathleen, that random guy she met and promised a date to, remember? She'd already passed away when he came around."

Catherine gaped. Suddenly everything had fallen into place. She pointed accusingly at Kenneth. "You've been around from the beginning!"

"Afraid so," he said indifferently. "Certainly took you a long time to figure out. I really thought you were smarter than this."

She tried to swallow and speak simultaneously but choked as a result before managing to pull out of her astonishment. "Why?"

"I'd had my eye on you for months at the museum, as I told you before. You never noticed me or any of the security guards."

"But why me? If you wanted that relic, why not stalk one of the others? I wasn't the whole museum staff."

"I started to," he said with a shrug. "But I quickly found out you were the one with the most knowledge and authority in the department I wanted."

Catherine frowned. "And my sister?"

"Accident. I thought she was you at first when I saw her and planned a 'chance meeting.'"

Bella let out a disgusted snort, and Catherine deepened her frown.

"You tricked both of my sisters, and attacked one of them, all for a relic?" Danny growled.

"It really was a complete lie between us. I was right not to trust you," Bella mumbled.

"I admit to it all," he responded proudly.

Catherine shot Bella a look when her friend let go of her hand and held her hands imploringly in front of her. "What now, Ken? What is all of this for?"

"The relic was destroyed," Catherine added.

He looked from one distraught woman to the next. "Do you think I'm an idiot? I know the relic is gone. I've been using Bella to find you and gather information."

"I never told him anything about you," she said quickly, glancing at Catherine out of the corner of her eye.

"She didn't have to. I overheard enough, and what I didn't, I stole from her phone. That is, until she broke it off with me."

"How dare you!" Bella threw her hands down.

"For God's sake, man. What the hell do you want?" Danny demanded.

"Power," he replied. Catherine couldn't keep the look of

profound revulsion off her face. He boldly stared back at her, unfazed. "Yours."

"What are you even thinking? You can't just take my power." She bit her lip. Now wouldn't be the best time to mention that someone else was already doing it.

"No I can't, but you can give it to me."

"He's insane," Danny said. "There's no point trying to make sense of it." He took Bella's hands in his and addressed his sister. "Let's just go. Just set him on fire if he tries to follow."

"I can't," she whispered. At least she didn't think she could so soon after Bricius. She didn't want to risk it unless she had no other choice.

"What? Why not?"

"Something's wrong," she muttered under her breath.

Kenneth chimed in. "Once again, I'm not an idiot," he said, sounding put upon. "I wouldn't attack you if I thought you had any defense against me. I know your power is faulty."

Catherine frowned again. "Yet you still want it?"

"Yes, because when it's out of you, it won't be drained anymore."

He can't know. How could he? "What?" she hissed.

"Could it be a certain missing stone?"

He knew, and she couldn't hide her dismay. She realized she'd been holding her breath, and exhaled deeply. "You know where it is?"

"Mhmm. But this can all be over if you relinquish your magic to me."

"Even if I could, I would never give it to you in a million years." She closed her fingers into tight fists at her sides.

"Not even to save the love of your life? Or Mary?"

Catherine's heart clenched, and her throat tightened at the mention of them. She shivered with rage at the fact that he would threaten his own blood. She didn't have to wonder what things he would say if she told him Mary was dead. And Bowen . . . she couldn't go there right now. Standing perfectly still, she squeezed her fists even tighter. "This is another trick."

"Afraid not. You see, I have the favor of one side of the fae war. If I wish it, they will slaughter anyone and everyone in that cottage."

"They're already dead, both of them!" Catherine shouted.

The news didn't seem to affect him in the slightest. "Then they'll hunt these two." He smiled at her companions.

Bella and Danny shifted and looked at each other nervously before looking at her. Catherine didn't move, frozen in her panic. She had no idea what she should do. What could she do to remove them from this cycle of nightmares?

"What'll it be?" he barked.

Catherine narrowed her eyes at him. Actually, she did know what she could do. "I'll yield."

"No!" Bella and Danny said in unison. They reached for her, but she batted them away without taking her eyes off Kenneth.

In silent approval, Kenneth nodded and dropped Bella's heavy locks. They fell with a thud to the forest floor. "Come on then."

Catherine turned to Bella and Danny. "Just get home."

"But—" Danny started.

She flatly shook her hand at her side, stopping Danny in his protest. Then, reluctantly, she took Kenneth's outstretched hand. She knew she couldn't trust him to keep his word, but she had to take the risk of throwing herself into the fire so they could have a chance to get away.

16

THE LONGER THEY WALKED, hand locked around arm, the more Kenneth seemed like the same crazed man Catherine had been trapped with in the museum. He pulled at her wildly, painfully gripping her, all the while grumbling to himself. Only this time, there wasn't a chance Bowen was coming to rescue her. Her weakened brother and best friend couldn't help, and Mary was lying dead in her living room. She'd have to try to run when they were far enough from the others so he couldn't harm them if she escaped.

"So where are you gonna do it?" she asked. He was practically dragging her now. Even so, she was grateful he wasn't looking at her long enough to see her thoughts skitter across her face. Among them, one sly notion lingered. Maybe she could distract him somehow. If she remembered correctly, he was easily riled up.

"Huh?" He was looking around frantically, as though missing something. "What are you babbling about?"

"We both know how you plan to take my magic."

He huffed a small laugh. "Did some faerie reading, did we? I can't say I blame you. There isn't much else to do in that town but read, and Gran had enough dusty volumes to last a decade."

"Do I detect a tone?" Catherine raised her eyebrows a notch. For a split second she thought there was a hint of familial affection next to the reluctance, but hidden behind the measured indifferent cadences he'd broadcasted.

"What?"

Catherine scowled. "You can't admit you miss Mary, can you?"

"No, because believe me, I don't. Now shut it."

"Let me tell you something, now that we're far enough away from the others," she said, wincing. His rough hold was chafing her arm. "You mistranslated Mary's books." He slowed his pace but didn't stop or look at her. She'd gotten his attention.

"She told me before she died that you couldn't have gained her magic if you killed her because you missed one important translation."

"Shut up, I'm tired of hearing your voice. You're just stalling."

"Yeah, that's right, and killing me won't give you my magic unless I consent to it. Once again, you'll be out of power but with another notch of damning evil on your belt."

Kenneth spun around, pushing his face into hers. "Lies! You're a liar!" he screamed and shook her violently. His bulging, wild eyes were all she could focus on.

Releasing her with a shove, he gripped his hair with both hands until it stood on end. "I need that power, they promised it to me!"

Catherine balanced herself and made sure to keep her distance. "Who promised you?"

Kenneth started, as though suddenly surprised by her presence, as if he'd forgotten she was there. He gave a mocking laugh.

"Who?" she pressed.

"I lost my chance to take Gran's magic, and now I've failed to steal from you."

Catherine frowned. What was he trying to say? Absentmindedly rubbing her pained lower back, she felt the hidden dagger. Mary's dagger. She'd forgotten about it, and amazingly, the blade hadn't damaged her or her jeans.

"I came to find the fae. I thought maybe they would help me get what I want. It's in my blood to want power. I thirst for it every second of every day."

He really was crazy. Her voice came out wobbly. "You're insane."

Kenneth continued as though she hadn't spoken. "I was taken to Loïc. He was going to kill me, but before he tried, I told him about the lock of hair you exchanged and the kind of power you wielded. I told him that the sun favored you like a lover, and so one loyal fae proclaimed he would blot out the healing rays as often as possible to keep you weak."

"What?" *How did he know?* Then she remembered he'd been spying on Bella. He may have also been the messenger who lit the fire on this faerie civil war she was blamed for. "You drew their attention to me."

"At first he didn't believe me," he continued without even a blink.

"Because he only believes Judicaël and me," said a woman's voice, silvery and devious. A bell-like note followed by an intrusive cawing came from somewhere in the trees. Catherine ducked as the sound of beating wings moved above her head. A crow landed on the path a short distance from where they stood. The gray and black hooded bird stared her down in a familiar way. Catherine shifted uncomfortably. It twitched and phased in and out of reality for a brief moment before a taller being, much more enticing to behold, stood in its place. Gwenaël.

"That's right, my gorgeous," Kenneth said between smiling lips, his demeanor now drastically calmer.

Catherine felt fire roaring in her eyes. She wouldn't let her guard down. The fae queen glided to Kenneth and, wrapping her long graceful arms around his neck, pulled him into a sensuous kiss. Catherine grimaced. The sight was not only sickening but bizarre. The queen towered over Kenneth, and standing right next to him as if molded to him, she looked nothing like a human. The fire continued to rage inside Catherine. Her list of problems wouldn't stop growing. She wished she could blow them both up and end this, but that would mean diminishing her magic. Not to mention Loïc and his court had the oathing stone. Without her protection spell, she couldn't risk wasting her fire. Not for these two.

Finally, they broke for air. "My, you're a transparent little thing, aren't you?" Gwenaël whispered.

Catherine glowered at them. She needed to steer Kenneth's mind back. Information was key. "Where is Loïc now?" Saying his name made her wish she could bring out his golden feather without them catching sight.

Gwenaël didn't meet her eyes. Eventually, Kenneth turned to look at her, and a deep frown spread across his face. "Once Loïc finally decided to believe me, he explained Judicaël's law. Human hair is contraband, especially from a druid. Cadeyrn shouldn't have kept it. I guess the power of each strand was too alluring for him."

Catherine fought back her growing frustration. "I am really tired of your monologue. Where is he?"

"Then he promised me I could kill you and take your power," Kenneth said, his trembling voice an octave lower. His cheeks flushed a shade darker.

Loïc had obviously led him on in an attempt to get what he wanted. Catherine couldn't understand why devious Kenneth was struggling with this revelation. She rested her hands on the backs of her hips, her palms itching for the hilt of her dagger. Would he ever communicate normally again? She didn't have the patience for this.

"If I can't have your power," he growled, eyes flashing, "or get revenge on your dried-up doctor, or on my gran for deceiving me, then I'll make sure you pay another way."

"You're the one who needs to pay for what you've done," she snapped.

Gwenaël caressed Kenneth's face, but he ripped out of her embrace. Catherine braced herself as he stomped toward her, kicking up dirt. She gasped as he shoved her, and struggled to stay standing. He was much bigger than she was. She swung her fists, but it was futile.

Catherine felt her pulse racing. She could ignore to some extent the personal threats, harassment, and berating, but he was seriously too crazy to run from. He shoved her one final time, and she groaned as her body painfully slammed into the nearest tree.

He stalked over as though he were a hunter and she was the deer he'd already shot. He slammed his hands down on either side of her head, his nose an inch away from hers.

"Get out of my face!" she screeched, and thrust Mary's dagger into his abdomen, pushing him backward.

A look of pure shock crossed his face. Catherine exhaled with relief and watched with satisfaction as blood began staining his clothes. Had Mary given her the dagger for this very reason? Kenneth stepped backward, one foot behind the other, past Gwenaël, who was showing no sign of any emotion whatsoever. He came to a standstill in the middle of the wide path.

The sound of powerful galloping fell on Catherine's ears before a giant black horse appeared on the path. Its spectral rider was headless. Right away, she knew—a Dullahan. Before she could blink the horse took off again, and a moment later, the rider swept Kenneth's head off in one clean motion. Catherine caught sight of something dangling on the saddle, lighting the phantom path that horse and rider disappeared into. Kenneth's head was still rolling.

Gwenaël glided away, completely unaffected by the demise of her lover, whose body was sprawled on the forest floor. Catherine's stomach lurched at the sight, and she turned away. In a dark way, she was pleased to know he'd gotten what he deserved, but the unsightly remains were nothing she wanted so vividly in her memory.

Gallop, gallop.

Catherine froze momentarily. The rider was coming back. She took off as fast as she could, the thunderous sound splitting the air behind her. She soon caught up with the silvery queen only to trip on one of the long, flowing attachments of Gwenaël's gown. Catherine felt herself falling in slow motion. She was falling through the faerie queen, who had suddenly become a ghost. Even though her body was falling slowly, her mind was on fast forward. She couldn't think. Just before she hit the slow-approaching ground, a strong arm scooped her up across her middle, and the next thing she knew, she was swiftly passing the trees in midair.

17

Catherine was flying. At least that's what it felt like until her dizzy senses came into focus. No, she wasn't flying. She was being carried. The large arm that held her firmly to the saddle on the wild horse squeezed so tightly she felt her ribs would break with a flick of the Dullahan's strong fingers.

The Dullahan was an Irish fae creature of death. He was clad completely in black, and—daring to look—she saw he carried his head on the other side of the saddle she was trapped against. Sparks from the horse's snorting nostrils pelted her. She could feel the raging steed's muscles moving rapidly beneath her. Her constantly slipping hand struggled to prop her up.

Catherine couldn't see a way out. Growing up, she'd heard the numerous Irish folklore stories of such a creature. She'd always enjoyed the fascinating tales spun mostly by local elderly storytellers. Each proclaimed at least one sighting, but these were always accounts of witnesses who'd watched from afar, or stories told after the fact. Never had Catherine imagined she'd be picked up by the legendary creature. She tried to remember any tales of people being taken to their deaths, but couldn't. All had died soon after being marked by the Dullahan. It would often mark its victims by blinding them with its whip or soaking them in a basin of blood. Kenneth's death had been quick. He'd been spared from the fear she was now condemned to. As poetic an Irish tale as this would be, she would rather not be the subject of it.

The horse burst into a large clearing and Catherine stifled a gasp. Clumped masses of all manner of fae were at each other's throats across the vast grasslands. The headless horseman charged straight through them, and several fae were killed by their opponents at the exact moment he passed. The arm around her tightened, and she strained to look up even though she was terrified of what she might see hanging high from the other arm. Beady, sunken eyes in a detached head looked around and then down at her, and a leering, hideous grin spread wider, touching both sides of the head. Catherine shivered as the banshee's warning of death came screeching back to mind.

None of the battling fae touched the Dullahan, but out of ignorance it seemed, rather than fear. It was almost as if they didn't notice him. The fae reined in the horse to a dirty, grinding halt, and Catherine lurched forward painfully, still in his hold. *Am I splitting apart?* she wondered vaguely through the pain. A rumbling call erupted from his chest. She grabbed her ears but could still hear the names he yelled.

Several heads rolled across their path at the exact moment that something spooked the steed, and it reared up on its hind legs. Catherine fell to the ground and scuffled only a second before bolting through the mayhem. She glimpsed behind her as the Dullahan lashed out his spine whip, but the pointed tip missed her by a hair, and she fled further out of reach. Much to her relief, she didn't hear any thunder.

The battle was colossal, ranging from the woods to the fields to the hills, as far as she could see. Catherine couldn't hide completely from the fight, but she managed to wedge herself between a cluster of trees leading up one of the giant rocks that speckled the clearing. Unable to completely catch her breath, she took in her surroundings. There really was no way out. Fae she'd never heard of or imagined battled each other in the surrounding woods and spread out across the open lands. A lake set in the middle of the neighboring valley was covered with them as if it were frozen, but even from her vantage point of cautiously peering from the tall rock, she could see rippling water beneath the skirmish.

A large, hulking fellow was run through with a glimmering sword right in front of her. The victor was short and covered completely with brown hair, no clothing. She pivoted on her perch to hide sideways behind the rock, careful with her footing on the precarious branches that webbed it. One last branch lay behind her before a drop to the field, but climbing up or hanging down from it was an unsettling prospect. It took everything in her not to make a sound or move to run, for if she did, this killer would give chase. She didn't have time to think about this for long. She didn't even have a chance to yelp when someone grabbed her shoulder from behind. Lips pressed abruptly on hers. Eyes wide open, she saw Cadeyrn looking back.

Catherine unceremoniously shoved him away, and he lithely met the last branch with ease. "Why did you do that?" she uttered hoarsely.

"You would have screamed," he said plainly.

She blinked a few times, staring at this strange human-like creature.

He flung his garments behind him. "I sensed you were here. I urge you to fight. Help me win the battle."

Catherine glowered at him, remembering what she'd recently learned. "This isn't my problem. My family and I shouldn't be in the middle of this."

"You're just as involved as I," he said calmly. "You know what is right. The fight has been brought to you, and defense isn't working. Strike back."

She scowled. "Why should I trust anything you say? I know you gave Loïc my oathing stone and caused all of this to happen to me."

He drew back with a look of shock. "That's absurd. I didn't know you had an oathing stone! That must be what he's using to drain your power." He shook his head. "I'm so foolish. I should have known he would track down the owner of the lock to figure out a way to gain more power than me."

"No, Bricius and Kenneth told me you did," she said angrily. "Besides, aren't you just using me for my power? Admit it. You wanted the lock!"

"Bricius? Bricius is Loïc's loyal spy who skulks in my court under the guise of honor. He has never known anything I didn't want him to pass on. I had hoped Loïc's knowing about the lock would discourage him from continuing against Judicaël, but I was wrong. It only pushed him to take action faster." He inhaled and exhaled deeply. "I am drawn to your power, I admit it. It can't be helped. Your hair wasn't something easily resisted when the opportunity you gave to us presented itself."

She felt Cadeyrn's convincing words encircle her, but still. "If I fight, it benefits your side."

"It is our side, druid woman."

Two stubby-legged male fae suddenly took to swords just above them on the rock. The clang and slide of the blades screeched down toward where they perched. "But how can I know that for sure?" she asked, and ducked with Cadeyrn right when a sword swiped down from above and barely missed them as they bobbed out of a slashed branch's path, tumbling between them. "What reason can you give me to join this war instead of escaping it?"

A stream of green fire shot through the entangled tree trunks and met with Cadeyrn's broadsword to bounce off and sear another fae down on the field through the chest. He turned a sound gaze back to Catherine. "It will stop Loïc, and bring a decade's worth of frowns to Judicaël."

He'd said the magic words. "Give me a weapon."

"Your magic?"

"I'm afraid to use it on its own. Give me a fae weapon to amplify it."

Cadeyrn unhooked a small metal rod piece off the ornamental jewelry hanging from his sleeve, and when he closed it in his palm, he righted it as a tall staff grew from it instantly. Light drew her eye to the top where two uneven shiny blades finished its crafting. He handed her the glaive. "Will this work?" he asked. She couldn't help but snort with a small grin. The glaive kept choosing her.

"Aye," she said, channeling Mary. Minding her footing, she turned to face the all-consuming battlefield. She would take part in this war until the opportune moment to escape it presented itself.

Cadeyrn wrapped his arm around her waist and turned her to face him once more. She looked up at him, mesmerized. On his breath was the scent of music. *How is that possible?* Its fragrance was elegant and empowering. "Victory," floated off his tongue, and with that he broke away down the drop into battle, leaving her hazy and breathless.

I've kissed or been kissed by a spy and two kings now, she thought with a mirthless laugh. The only lips she'd ever yearned for were probably cracked and cold by now, but her adrenaline refused to let her feel the heartache. Instead, her heart beat with the rushing thrill of a life-or-death battle. Instinct took over. She was going to live for as long as breath would keep her.

Using the glaive as leverage, she moved in a wide leap forward. As she flung herself out from the safety of the shade, she thrust her weapon through a tattooed giant blocking out the sunlight only feet away. He was at least five times her size, and she slashed down from his neck to his groin, using the glaive to slow her descent. She met the ground wide-legged, and pulled it out of him in a twisting dance. The fae fell to his knees before toppling over into the rock and loudly snapping the trees behind her. She didn't look back. She would never look back. The sun was high in the sky now, and it favored her. Was the sun her only lover now?

Following her instinct and not her eyes, Catherine flung herself into the swing of the glaive, jabbing a neighboring enemy in the gut then slashing sideways to meet another. She screamed her war cry as fae blood sprinkled her face and soaked the front of her clothes. She jumped nimbly aside and onto the backs of two corpses where she met the gaze of a hairy, squinty-eyed brute. His companions formed a circle around her. A cowardly scare tactic. *Pathetic.*

The leader howled like a wild hound, while the two flanking him snarled. Grossly large jaws dripped pools of foaming drool, and with a sickening crunch of his robust knuckles, the leader chuckled. Unaffected, Catherine summoned a thread of her magic and watched as it latched in coils over the length of the faerie glaive. The chuckling fool drew her gaze back, and she crouched. They all moved now, circling her slowly, as though in a game of cat and mouse. She smiled a devilish smile. *Now.*

She thrust the magic glaive into the howler, and bright, burning lava instantly seeped out of the wound. His scream stuck in his throat. Before the others could jump she finished the job, slashing him in half. Using her momentum, she continued to spin, piercing every belly and torso in the circle. With her enemies down, she dug the rounded bottom of her weapon into the ground beside her, holding it like a staff. The blade pointed to the skies, aglow with liquid fire and glazed in blood. She was a war goddess, and she claimed this fae mound. The ground bubbled lava. The fool didn't laugh anymore.

She was an animal, given over completely to instinct. She would let her soul hide while her body was consumed with magic, fire, and boiling blood. A riveting communion.

Something suddenly sparked on the side of her head, breaking her focus, and she slapped it repeatedly to put it out.

At that moment Cadeyrn unleashed a bellowing war cry. He was standing some distance away, on his own mound of fae corpses. In one hand his broadsword glowed, while in the other he held something aloft, victoriously. Halos of smoke spewed from his uplifted hand, spiraling high above him. Catherine inhaled deeply. The smoke wove itself into her and set itself behind her eyes, and then she knew. It was the lock.

She ran to him, sensing another part of her power calling out, avoiding enemies but destroying those who dared get in her way. He fastened his gaze on her as she reached him. She knew he could feel her presence. Somehow activating as he held it, the lock's power connected them. One of his eyebrows twitched. "I told you I could sense you."

"Why are you using it?" she shouted over the chaos around them. "I thought you weren't going to use me!"

"I'm not," he boomed. She felt his powerful voice radiate through her. *Then what is this?* she wanted to say, but he already knew. "I'm destroying it. We should never have had it."

The hand clasped to the lock looked sheer white and spotted with glass. As she stood next to him, their enemies swirling around them, the lock disappeared into one last puff of smoke. He opened his hand, and clear liquid ran down the length of his arm. The lock was finished.

Lightheaded, Catherine stumbled backward before the king grabbed her. Her energy, melded with Mary's, was waning. *The oathing stone.* She had to get it back, the only thing she had left of her beloved. She had to hurry.

"Fight," Cadeyrn said in her ear before leaving her side. She wobbled but stood her ground as an enemy fae approached.

Facing the skies, pulling what she could from the sunlight on her skin, she called a ball of flame into her empty palm. She shot it out into his path as she sidestepped his attack, but he was too strong, and she was too weak. Her fireball extinguished on contact and steamed the rest of the way into his icy exterior. His blue eyes had rings of black around the edges that projected confusing flashes. She weaved and bobbed like a boxer until one large flash sent her flat on her back. *This is it,* she thought. Suddenly, the end of a javelin pierced his head, and he fell over half on top of her. She wrestled with some difficulty to get out from under him, his frosted skin burning her like dried ice. Regaining freedom with the aid of a nearby shield, she retrieved her glaive and pressed forward. She needed to get out of there and get her oathing stone. *Find Loïc.*

Cadeyrn could have the rest of the war. She had full confidence he'd never needed her help and could win it entirely on his own. Or maybe she was a little muddled. Why did everything look as though it were coming at her from the end of a long tunnel? She needed to retain her strength, to regain her full power by finding the one who had it, and close this quarrelsome realm off. Somehow she was sure Loïc was somewhere on or around the battlefield, like she could sense it.

Reaching a border of the battle that wasn't as heavily occupied, she followed the jutting rocks pushing up from the ground in a line through the fields. Some ended just inside lush woods where she stopped running. The wind blew vibrant leaves into rhythmic fits, and they reached back to caress the wind with affection. With no one immediately around to attack, she pulled the feather out of her pocket. Its golden glow grew brighter every second.

Something familiar tainted the air. A melody. A special wind force all its own. It floated over to the trees as if to say hello before floating downward, closer to Catherine.

"Loïc," she said.

18

As if on cue, he appeared on the forest floor before her in a swirl of twigs and grass. The music ceased. "In my wildest dreams, I never imagined that you would last as long as you have, druid woman."

Catherine really wished the fae would stop calling her that.

Perfectly poised, Loïc narrowed his hellish yellow and black eyes. "Give up."

"Never." She jabbed her glaive into the earth and leaned on it heavily. "I've come to face you."

"Face me?" He laughed, his face full of pure hatred. "You can barely stand."

"If you hate me so much, why did you lure me to your realm?"

"I didn't. I've detested every second you've been here. I hate humans. I was already taking your power, and I would have had it all by now if you hadn't come here, even with the protection magic you burned into your flesh. In fact, as soon as you passed the threshold from your realm to mine, the process slowed."

"Give me what's mine," she demanded.

"I am a king."

"A thief," she corrected.

"Your impertinence annoys me." He glided casually closer and tilted his head. The golden feathers in his headdress rustled. "I tried to get rid of Cadeyrn. He's the only one of the lower kings who wouldn't listen to me, the foolish whelp."

Feeling her patience wearing into the thinnest of layers, Catherine could only stare at him.

"All the others agreed to serve me as their new high king, and with Judicaël out of the way, what could stop me?" He sighed. "Not anyone. I've been planning this for centuries, meticulously planting my seeds, whispering in every ear, until what happens? You and that damn lock. Suddenly Cadeyrn is more interesting in Judicaël's eyes, and an enormous thorn in my side."

"So you turned Judicaël against him, and set the civil war into full swing." Loïc grimaced and snarled at her, but she persisted. "I'm not sorry to have spoiled your plans, but it isn't my fault he's fighting against you—"

"It is your fault! You disgusting druid woman, so easily finding favor with two kings. Makes me sick," he spat.

She clenched her jaw and balled her free hand into a fist. "Cadeyrn is winning, and without my lock of hair. You underestimated him." She wanted nothing more than to end this.

Twisting his face into a deeper frown, Loïc didn't reply. Instead, he lifted his hands in front of him. Catherine took half a step forward and restrained a gasp. In one of his long, elegant palms sat the stone. He rolled it around between both hands, playing with it, taunting her.

"Return it," she said, voice low, eyes furious. She straightened as air burst through her pores. It shot her hair on end then settled into steam around her.

"Never," he said, mimicking her. "Thanks to my spy it's been my key, my way to defeat Cadeyrn and his lock, allowing me to finally overthrow Judicaël." He sneered. "I already have all the ancient power from that dead man. It's you who's been taking far too long."

At the mention of Bowen, her fire within raged in a blazing fury, and she let out a riotous scream.

"Oh, yes, please. Please use all of that stored-up magic and I can finish you off with a flick of my finger." His lips curved into a malevolent smile.

Closing her eyes, Catherine ignored his oppressive presence as best she could. Being so close to the oathing stone, she could feel it draining her while also calling out to her. She needed to focus all of her concentration on keeping her strength and listening to the stone. *Now.* Her eyes shot open, and she speared the glaive at Loïc. The glaive found its target in his side, swiftly knocking her prize off his open palm.

Before he could move to retrieve it, she launched herself onto him, dropping the glaive in the process, and they tumbled away from the stone. He shoved her away with a look of disgust. *Oh no, you don't.* Catherine slammed her hands onto his face and dug in her nails as hard as she could. Grappling with her arms, he tried to pry her away. *Not as weak as you thought!* As she let the fire burst through her palms, still attached to him, his voice turned into a mind-throbbing screech.

Though she wanted to finish him and boil his insides, she resisted. With one last shove, she lifted herself off him and lunged toward the stone. It was smooth, warm to the touch. It was hers again. Even as she stood there, Catherine felt the fires returning, melting into her bones as they grew stronger.

She sighed with pleasure and relief. She had reversed the process. Glancing at Loïc with a victorious smile on her face, she started. His expression was that of unthinkable rage. She didn't even see it coming. Her lungs constricted as some powerful force rammed into her back, knocking her to the ground near her glaive. The stone fell out of her hands back into the dirt.

Loïc lunged again. Leaping back to her feet, glaive in hand, Catherine propelled herself over and behind him. Landing, she thrust the blade into his spine and slashed upward. As his body fell forward to the ground, the air around it smudged and shifted, back into the black-clothed fae she knew as a shapeshifter.

Something told her to move, so she listened and turned around in time to face the real Loïc. Before she knew what was happening, he'd knocked the glaive out of her hands and was strangling her. She couldn't cough or move as she felt her life being choked out of her. Avoiding his eyes, she looked past him. She would not let this hateful creature be the last thing she saw.

Her vision tunneled, and she couldn't think straight enough to summon her fires. Large piles of leaves suddenly began falling from the trees directly in view, and swirling winds rushed in to scoop them up and spread them out. Then she heard it, that distant wailing. It might have happened in an instant, or it might have just seemed like it. The banshee appeared from thin air and grabbed Loïc by the neck, pulling him away. Catherine doubled over and snatched up the glaive. By the time she'd run Loïc through, straight in the chest, his body was already devoid of life and hung limply in the banshee's clutches. The faerie woman gave a shriek that curdled all blood within earshot.

She leaned in so that her shapely lips just barely brushed Loïc's ear. "I do not mourn for you," she said, her voice ice cold, and then dropped him like a garbage bag. The beautiful wailing woman stepped over the body and approached Catherine. "It is finished."

Catherine looked at her, stunned. "Why did you save me?"

"I didn't. I came to kill Loïc."

Catherine parted her lips to speak but then remembered that the banshee didn't like too many questions. "I dropped the feather somewhere around here," she mumbled, cocking her head as she scanned the ground.

The fae woman slowly shook her head. "No need, leave it lost."

Catherine was about to respond when, spotting the oathing

stone near her on the ground, she quickly picked it up and stuffed it deep in a pocket of her jeans. "Thank you anyway, and hopefully we'll never see each other again."

The banshee nodded eerily, but Catherine was already turning around to prepare for what was next.

19

CATHERINE SPRINTED across and bounded over every obstacle of the forest, including discarded pieces of fae armor and weaponry. The number of corpses thinned out the further she went. She was so close, she could feel she just had to push a little longer. The feeling of her power healing and flowing stronger gave her more confidence with each passing minute. Finally, she reached the border. Her blood-glazed glaive clattered loudly against the rocky ground behind her as she cast it aside to join the other scattered arms. Catherine passed through the fae realm and into the human realm. She'd made it. She was home.

It was time to put everything she had into this last hurdle. She hoped with every dream within a dream, and every hope on her sleeve, that Bella and Danny had survived and made it out in time. She had to finish this. Only then could she let herself give up and die.

She felt hot tears streaming down her face as she turned and stared ahead, back at the faerie realm. With an unfailing gaze, she pushed her will into the air. It surrounded the tree directly in front of her, then another tree, then the next tree after it until after what seemed an eternity had passed. She'd extended her gaze farther across the faerie lands than she ever had. She struggled to contain the power within her while also seeking to expand it as far as possible. As the strain began to push her body to its limits, she fell to her knees in the dirt and braced herself, hands planted in front and both arms locked. Catherine let her head hang between them. Sweat bubbled along her neck and brow, the latter occasionally twitching in concentration.

She had to close it. The faerie world was too dangerous, and they were coming for her power. How many other humans would they harm? She wouldn't allow it. The fae needed to be cut off, and remain that way for a millennium or more. She quickly pushed the thought of Bowen away. She couldn't let herself think of where Bowen's spirit had gone, or of his limp body in their bed. Or of Mary's dead one on the living room couch. She was alone, and she had to do it, no matter the cost. Even if she lost everyone she had dared love.

"I'm here."

Catherine's heart jumped. It couldn't be.

"It's me."

She crumpled her doubts into a tiny ball and let herself believe. It was Bowen's voice but it sounded distant, and she didn't hear it with her ears. "How?"

"I haven't the faintest idea, but here I am. I'm still in the fae lands, almost out."

"You need to get out now! I'm shutting the fae realm off from ours, and it's already started. I can't stop it!"

"I'm almost there," he growled, panting.

As if sensing her fear, the wave of magic picked up speed and began moving of its own will. Catherine shook her head violently. "You're not gonna make it. I'm coming in!"

"No!"

"Hurry!"

She could feel it—it tingled in her skin and pulled at her mind

—every last tree, leaf, petal, and shard of grass. All soil and air beloved by the fae was caught in her web of magic.

"Are you out?"

Cold silence.

"Bowen!"

Life-giving fire surged through her veins, and its return was equivalent to a thousand firecrackers bursting across the sky. Unable to delay another minute, Catherine released the fire from her palms. The tongues licked at each other spitefully until they extended enough to connect and form a crimson beam of light. She turned her palms in on each other, struggling to contain the heavy energy. Her arms and hands shook, and then with great force, she slammed them flat on the ground in front of her at the threshold of the fae realm.

The approaching wave of energy swept over the sky to reveal a world locked in a bubble, a world slowly being erased from the earth. The dome-shaped magic lingered at the top of the curve in uneven strokes that resembled creeping pools of liquid before plunging downward, regaining speed. A nearby rustling caught her ear. Barely managing to hold on to her magic's overwhelming will, she glanced toward it through squinted eyes, hoping to see her husband's ghost. There was nothing but the forest, where her delusions of him had phased in and out.

Her desire to let go of the power and shout out to him in warning was almost overpowering. Maybe there was a chance he could still hear her.

The speeding cage fell in an instant, cutting through the air like a guillotine.

The yellow ball rising from the horizon bled every shade of red, orange, and yellow with tiny rivers of color weaving in and out of thin clouds. Catherine stood in its first light, staring wide-eyed into the forest.

"Bowen?" Catherine waited a second. "Bowen, please!" She

waited again, but she knew that no matter how much she wanted to, she couldn't deny that the voice was gone. He was gone.

The black forest was no longer blackened by the mark of the fae but filled with colorful morning light. For the first time, the forest was allowed to kiss the sky hello as if it were greeting a dear old friend.

But the beauty was lost on her. "No." She choked back the sobs and the rising hysterics already threatening her sanity. She would finish this. She could always die later.

She had to make sure there wasn't any breach, nothing left to get in or out of the fae realm. She hurried along what used to be the borderline between the realms, carefully examining the grounds as she went until she happened upon a sight that made her draw back in horror. An involuntary gasp escaped her mouth. On top of the green, just by her feet, lay a hand, unattached from a body. The grass beneath it was stained with blood, but past a defined line, the grass remained untainted. The hand had been cut cleanly, right at the wrist. Obviously it had been seared off by the magic border.

Squatting down, careful not to touch it, Catherine looked it over. Masculine and rugged with slender fingers. She grabbed at her chest, trying to control her sudden rapid breathing, and clamped her eyes shut. One of the two men who held her heart was handless, and both might be lost to her forever.

Catherine knew she couldn't restrain or control the grief beating inside herself much longer. She rose from her crouched position and walked away from the bloodied hand, fighting desperately to ignore the haunting impression it had left on her mind. On she went around the border. It could take days, but she was determined. Then a few yards away from the hand, she collapsed facedown in the green, unconscious.

Catherine woke to a prickling on her skin, and reflexively slapped at the grass swaying on her arm in a passing breeze. How much time had passed? She stood on wobbly legs and stared blankly at the Irish fields and forests. The distant rolling hills seemed to smile at her. No thoughts ran through her tired, fuzzy mind. She scarcely noticed the wind knocking at her battered clothing. Her headscarf fell out of her pocket before it was swiftly swept up by the breeze and blew gently to her feet, and she looked at it curiously. She couldn't seem to move her thoughts past what was happening around her. There was a deep, burrowing feeling in the pit of her stomach and an unbearable ache in her heart. Something was evading her, or she was evading it. Whatever it was, she needed to get it out.

Without warning, Catherine felt her lungs inhale air painfully before releasing themselves in a violent coughing fit that nearly knocked her over. Everything came crashing down around her. *Bowen, Danny, Bella. Bowen. Bowen!* She cried out and wept between the coughs choking her. She spun around and launched herself into motion, past the hand, back to where she'd locked the faerie realm away. She had to pull the bubble back, bring the cage back and break it.

Her cheeks burned with tears as she tried to summon her magic. She swirled her arms and kicked her legs, releasing cries that weaved in and out of tortured screams. No matter how hard she tried, she could not undo what she had sealed. She was already going mad, and she was dangerous to the human world she had just sacrificed everything to protect.

With that thought, Catherine snapped herself out of her hysterics. She felt total clarity. She had to end herself. Without his body, Bowen would soon follow. She wouldn't be alone for long. She turned on her heel but stopped short, shock stealing her breath.

Bowen, body and soul, was running toward her. It took half a second for her to accept she wasn't delusional before she picked up her wobbly knees and ran with shaking legs. The wind was rising, and like an actual hand, it pushed on her back. With each step she found renewed strength and hope, and then they crashed into each other in a mess of sobs and relief.

"I'm really touching you, Bowen! It's really you! You're alive!"

"I got here before you died. That's all that matters!"

Catherine smashed her body to his until there was no room for more closeness, wrapping her arms around him. He did the same as they rocked each other back and forth in a soothing rhythm. She needed to feel him in her arms, to hold him as tightly as possible to slow her heart from its breaking speed. With each rocking motion, her heart mended a little more until it was only frayed along the edges. He was alive. He was here with her again. A waterfall of emotions coursed through her.

Soft, slow kisses grew passionate. Finally, their pantings ceased, and she pulled back enough to look deeply into his eyes. His face was thinner than before, but there was no longer any trace of the sallow or ashen skin. Another wave of relief crashed down on her, and more worries shattered against the rocks. "I nearly did die," she whispered. Oh, those perfect eyes, perfect pools of green, the ones she wanted to spend eternity gazing into.

"You can't die without me," he said, his voice raspy.

The sound of his voice. How she adored it. "I'll do my best." She smiled, and he returned it with one more kiss. "Why didn't you answer me when you got out?"

“As soon as I did I was back in my body at the cottage. I couldn’t reach out to you as I did in spirit.”

“You can’t imagine my relief, Bowen.”

“I think I can,” he replied with a large smile.

“Wait.” It dawned on her, and her chest tightened once more. “The hand—” She looked behind at the brightly lit forest, empty of Danny and Bella. They were now trapped in the faerie realm, and there was nothing she could do about it.

20

"HURRY!" Dan's shout echoed through the space and hung on Bella's pained ears. She could barely hear over her own heavy breathing as she tried to keep up. The hair was not helping matters. Hearing the thunder in the distance, they'd picked up their speed, moving in the direction Cathy had told her to go before the events leading to Ken dragging her dear friend away. They'd run until the thunder faded, sounding further and further away, but still they'd walked with as much haste as they could muster. They'd rested in five-minute increments, their eyes trained on every bend and corner.

Now, time felt as though it was actually passing through them, and the urge to rush was greater than the need to rest.

A man's whispering voice echoed through the trees. Alarmed, Dan stopped, and Bella followed suit. Everything went silent. He turned to look at her, his charming smile warming her heart as he caressed her cheek with one hand. She leaned into the caress and wrapped her arms around his waist. "Bella," he whispered.

"Hmm?" She groggily reopened her eyes.

"I'm going to run ahead. Follow me as best you can, but I want to make sure that voice wasn't a fae luring us into a trap."

"What? If it is, you'll fall into it."

"Yeah, but you will still have a chance if I do."

"Dan," she sobbed. "Do you remember what happened last time?"

"I was stupid. Yeah, I know, but this is different. It's a straight line, and you'll be able to see me the whole time."

Bella shook her head. "I don't feel right about this, but—"

"Hurry," he repeated. He slid his warm hands away and darted into the gloom.

Bella dashed after him. Through her misty vision, she saw something change in the skies, and a deep, worrisome pang in her stomach sent her rushing to catch up with Dan. He slipped through the air like a bullet. She'd forgotten just how athletic he used to be. Whatever was happening, she didn't want to be separated from him for even a second.

After having many hours and full days of struggling through the forest contending with her hair, she'd managed to pick up her speed. She amazed herself; her footing was truly skilled as she danced across the forest floor, avoiding each protruding hazard in her way. Her jaw set, and her eyes fixed ahead. The sound of her heavy breathing was all she heard. Determination marked itself on her, inside and out.

Soon Bella spotted the top of Dan's head weaving and bobbing far ahead. Should she yell and cease this mad chase? She shook her head as she continued to spring. He was still too far, and she couldn't risk losing sight of him. Instead, she kept her eye on the brown hair blowing out behind him. Her own locks were doing the same, streaming far behind her as though the winds were tugging on each strand in a jealous battle. She wondered if the wind was a fae. She would have never imagined it possible before she met Cathy, but she didn't care. The wind could take her belongings, her hair, even her image, but they would not take Dan from her.

Though her physical endurance was wearing thin, Bella could see she was gaining on him. With renewed motivation, she pushed on. Suddenly Dan's bobbing head dropped from sight. She picked up her pace even more. She could see him just ahead, lying face-down on the forest floor covered in dead leaves and grass. Bella gasped. The trees ended only a few steps away from where he'd plummeted. Home was within reach. She came to a screeching halt, burying her feet in the dirt. Tiny twigs and rocks rained against her legs. Her hair whipped violently against her bare back and arms, but the sensations barely registered. What worried her was the sky.

It was folding and crinkling loudly. Waves of light crashed over each other before spreading outward at rapid speed, as though hurtling themselves to the edge of a cliff.

Then the waves moved down. *The sky is actually falling,* Bella thought, panic rising. It was falling straight ahead, straight at Dan. She quickly closed the gap between them, grabbed onto the backs of both of his ankles and pulled with all her strength. The falling sky cut down between the edge of the forest and home, ending with a final *shring*. The resulting wild blast knocked her backward off her feet.

Bella scrambled her way back to her feet and was met with thick clouds of dust filling the air. Covering over her face as she coughed with one hand, and waving her way through it with the other, she managed to recognize where Dan was lying before stepping on him. "Dan?" He still hadn't gotten up, but his back was heaving. "Are you hurt?" No answer. Though afraid of what she might see, she crouched down and put her face close to his. Drenched in sweat, he seemed unconscious but under visible strain. His arms were still stretched out ahead, reaching for the way home. Bella tilted her head up, and as the dust clouds began to clear, she saw the fallen sky was a misty substance. A veil of some sort spread out on both sides from there, disappearing into the distances and gloom of the woods. Looking at it directly, she saw that it reflected back endless trees and an image of her and Dan.

"Dan?" she barely whispered. The forest was suddenly deathly quiet. The wind was gone and with it all the rattlings of nature.

Placing her hands on his tensed and shivering back and shoulders, she tried to roll him over. With a bit of a struggle she succeeded, and as his arms flopped back, she gasped in horror. Where his left hand should have been was a bloody stump.

Bella grabbed at her face and chest and then, falling out of her crouch, she wrapped her arms around her knees and rocked herself. She couldn't stop the moans. She was alone, Dan was wounded, and they were trapped. She gave herself over to her sobs. Cathy must have been dead, or they wouldn't be there.

Calming slightly, she wiped her dirty hands over her tear-streaked face. She had to find a way to hide Dan. Just as she began moving toward him, a rustling sound froze her in place. Her gaze snapped up. Just a few feet ahead was a tall man—no, he was a fae. His ghostly aura and beautiful features made that clear. She didn't say anything, and neither did he. They stared at each other as he slowly came forward. She couldn't tell if he was threatening or not but watched cautiously for a clue.

Dan groaned loudly, and from her gut shot the keenest pang she'd ever felt. Glancing back, she saw terrible realization dawn on his face, which twisted into a nightmarish grimace. His howls echoed hellishly in the misty woods.

With the help of Pastor Kelley, Catherine and Bowen gave their old friend a quiet and lovely funeral, with the town locals paying their respects. The next day, as per Mary's documented request, they sprinkled her ashes in the ruins she had loved the most. Her wish to be as human as possible, even in death, had been granted.

In the days that followed, Catherine tried to throw herself into managing all her new responsibilities. Mary had passed on all that she owned to her, including the shops in town, under Pastor Kelley's name to keep Catherine's life from outside interruption. Even with her heavy workload, Catherine could dwell only on her aching guilt. She needed to get away from it somehow but couldn't. Bowen was her only solace. Every day they would lie together on the greener portions of the ruin grounds.

Today, Catherine held the oathing stone in her hands, running her thumbs over its surface, both smooth and bumpy. She'd kept it with her ever since retrieving it. How many more times would she be faced so severely with mortality?

Bowen reached toward her gently and slowly took the oathing stone. "This time, we should give it to the sea."

She nodded absentmindedly. Danny and Bella were forever trapped in the faerie realm with its civil war. And Judicaël. And it was her fault. She knew she could never free them, there was no hope, but she prayed that they somehow knew how deep her sorrow ran and that if they were still alive and knew it had been her fault, they would grant her forgiveness someday.

"They have each other," Bowen said, interpreting her thoughts.

She turned to look up at him from where she lay back against his chest, comfortably sitting between his long legs. "But what if they don't? What if they're separated? Dead? Or being tortured? I don't know if I can live with myself like this, not knowing."

A flicker moved across his concerned eyes as he looked down at her imploring ones. He wouldn't be able to give her the answers she wanted, the answers she needed. Instead, his warm lips gifted her forehead a soft kiss. She closed her eyelids, and the salty sting behind them released itself as she pushed her head harder into the comforting curve of his neck.

"Bowen."

"Hmm?"

"You can't ever die."

"I'll do my best," he said with a chuckle.

"No, I mean it. I never want to hear a banshee's cry ever again."

The banshee was wrong. She lived.

ACKNOWLEDGMENTS

First, I want to thank my family and the Lord for their endless love and support that got me through every bad day and writing struggle. You are always my everything!

Specifically, I want to thank my husband, you've been my steady arm when I felt shaky. Thank you for the constant encouragement, love, and believing in me.

Thank you to my grandmother for your encouragement, friendship, and love.

To my many friends who've cheered me on, you are true friends to be there for me whether I'm unknown or known, starting out or improved. You're there when it counts, with honesty, mutual respect and kindness. Thank you for being you.

An enthusiastic thank you to Rachel Small for such an insightful developmental edit on this book! You helped me reveal the inner thoughts of my characters more often and in a better way. Your work made a tremendous difference for this story, and I couldn't be happier because of it!

I want to give a special thank you to my awesome street team! All of you have been fantastic, and I can never say enough words to describe how great you are. Especially, Haddie, Kim, Drew, and Alessa for always being so supportive with their excitement in my writing!

Thank you to my amazing copyeditor Candace Kuhn for the skillful and excellent work on my book, allowing me to polish it into a delightful finished product.

Thank you to Lavender Prose for the beta reads, and the proofread! You helped me show more of the world I've created, then polish it, and for that, I am eternally grateful.

Thank you to my forever lovely, kind, and talented cover artist Mélanie Delon. Your art style is always breathtaking, and you made Catherine and my book cover shine once more. I can't wait to see what you do with the final book in my trilogy!

Finally, thank you to my awesome and efficient print distributor Gatekeeper Press.

I'm incredibly thankful to every person who helped me in one way or another to make this book into what it is and known to readers.

To all my readers, old and new, thank you!

ABOUT THE AUTHOR

J.Z.N. McCauley is an award-winning fantasy author residing in lovely New England, where she loves wearing jackets and boots in the unpredictable weather there. She is a wife and mother who enjoys life to the fullest. Also, being a nerd across many fandoms is something she expresses openly.

McCauley spends most of her spare time writing, drawing, or reading. She loves archeology, mythology, history, music and many other forms of art as well. Always having a variety of interests and talents, she could never pick just one. When the chance pops up to travel to any of her favorite places, she takes way too many pictures. Otherwise, she is exploring a mystical land in a daydream, which all provides fuel to her immense joy of writing.

Among several works in progress, she is currently writing an epic fantasy series that she hopes will enchant readers as much as it has her.

Visit her Online at

www.jznmccauley.com

Instagram (@JZNMcCauley)

Twitter (@JZNMcCauley)

Facebook.com/JZNMcCauley

ALSO BY J.Z.N. MCCAULEY

A Bell Sound Everlasting

The Zinnia Queen

The Rituals Trilogy

Oak and Mistletoe

The Oathing Stone

www.ingramcontent.com/pod-product-compliance
Ingram Content Group UK Ltd.
Pitfield, Milton Keynes, MK11 3LW, UK
UKHW041839190726
13854UKWH00002B/618